The Basket of Flowers

by

Christoph Von Schmid

This editon of A Basket of Flowers
© copyright 1999
Reprinted 2001, 2003
Christian Focus Publications
ISBN:185792-525-4

Published by
Christian Focus Publications Ltd
Geanies House, Fearn ,Tain, Ross-shire,
IV20 1TW, Scotland, Great Britain.
www.christianfocus.com
email: info@christianfocus.com

Cover design by Catherine Mackenzie

Printed and Bound in Great Britain
by Cox & Wyman, Cardiff Road, Reading
Originally published by Lutterworth Press

This book is reprinted by request of people who have read and enjoyed this book in the past. *The Basket of Flowers* has been edited slightly to make the book more accessible to a new generation but the editorial we believe has been in keeping with the original style of the book and does not take away from the simplicity of the story and its message. We hope that this book will enjoy many more years of popularity as a result.

Contents

Father and Daughter

In a certain little market town in Guelderland, there lived more than a hundred years ago an upright and intelligent man named Jacob Rode. He had come there as a poor boy to learn the trade of gardening in the gardens of the castle of the Count of Terborg. His many excellent qualities of mind and heart, the readiness with which he set about everything he was asked to do, and it must be added, the frank and kindly expression of his face, attracted the attention of the noble family he served. He soon became a favourite with all its members and would be called upon to do many little duties in the castle. When the young Count, after finishing his studies, set out on his travels, Jacob was made one of his retinue. In the course of these wanderings the young man saw many strange cities and was brought in contact with people of different countries and habits. This enabled him to enrich his understanding by a great variety of knowledge. By mixing with cultured people, he also learned how to speak well and improve his manners. This meant that on his return to Terborg, he gave pleasure to those who knew him by the evident good use he had made of his opportunities for educational purposes. As well as that he brought back a heart and mind unspoiled by their contact with the great world.

During all this time Jacob had greatly impressed his master. When they reached home one of the Count's first thoughts was how best to reward his servant for his diligence and loyalty; after some consideration he decided to offer him the stewardship of his palace in the capital, which was a position of great trust and importance. Jacob, however, had no desire to live in the city; he had seen enough of them, and longed for a quiet, useful life in the country.

It happened that just at this time a small property belonging to the Count became vacant; it was just the kind of house Jacob desired and so he asked his master to let him have it. The Count, eager to reward his faithful servant, granted his request; but he was more generous than Jacob could have expected, for he allowed him to enjoy the place rent-free for as long as he lived, and in addition promised him as much corn and wood for his future household as would be required.

This to the humble-minded Jacob was a princely fortune, and enabled him to complete his happiness, as far as this world's goods are concerned, by marrying a virtuous young woman of Terborg with whom he was very much in love. His days now were spent in perfect calm and content. He rose early and worked late, tilling and taking care of his little property which was his for life. It consisted of a pleasant little house in the midst of a large garden, half of which was planted with fruit-trees, while the other half was laid out for vegetables.

After Jacob had lived many happy years with his wife, who was in every respect a most excellent woman, she was taken away from him by death. His pain at her loss was inexpressible. The good man, who was by this time getting old, aged visibly, and his hair grew daily whiter and whiter. Now, the only friend he had in the world was his daughter; she was the only one left of several children, and at her mother's death was but five years old. She was called Mary after her mother, of whom she was in all things a perfect image.

Even as a child Mary was uncommonly pretty; but as she grew in years her piety, her innocence, her modesty, and her unfeigned kindness towards all she came in contact with, gave her beauty a rare and peculiar charm. Before she was fifteen years of age, she was able to take the entire charge of her father's house; and never was a home better cared for. In the bright little living-room there was never a speck of dust to be seen; the pots and pans in the kitchen shone as if new, and the whole house was a pattern of order and cleanliness. Besides attending to all these things indoors, Mary managed to find time to help her father with the work in the garden, and the hours she spent with him out-of-doors were amongst the happiest of her life. For the old man, who had enriched his mind with knowledge and wisdom, was able, by his instructive and entertaining conversation, to make labour a pleasure and delight.

Mary had grown up in the midst of plants and flowers. Her whole world was the garden. From her earliest childhood she showed the greatest delight in flowers. Her father, therefore, each year would search out for her a few fresh seeds, roots, and cuttings. He would then allow her to plant these all round the edges of the beds in the garden. Mary loved to watch them grow. This was the occupation of her leisure hours, and it was the pleasantest of employments. Each little plant was tended with the greatest care; its growth and development were watched with increasing interest day by day, until, when the time came for the flower to unfold itself, her anxiety to see what it was like would almost get the better of her judgment; but, being schooled in self-restraint, she would wait with patience, and then, when the bud at last burst and disclosed the flower in all its beauty, her pleasure was indescribable.

Mary's father would say "Yours is a pure and innocent pleasure. Many parents give more shillings for jewellery and pretty dresses than I give pence for flower-seeds, and yet do not give their daughters one-half the pleasure that I give you."

What was more, for Mary fresh joys blossomed every month, even every week. Often she would exclaim in her delight: "The garden of the Castle itself can hardly be more beautiful than ours!"

It was indeed very beautiful, so beautiful that people as they passed by would stop and admire, praising the garden and the gardener. And children, as they went to and fro, could not help lingering and longing as they looked through the fence at the rich array of flowers. If Mary happened to see them, she would often send them on their way with a sweet posy of blossoms to carry home.

The wise father, however, while rejoicing to see his daughter take so deep a delight in flowers, knew how to turn her pleasure to a higher purpose. He taught her to see and admire in the beauty of flowers the unvarying goodness, wisdom, and omnipotence of God. He was accustomed to devote the first hour of the morning to devotion; and in order that the day's work need not be interfered with, he rose an hour earlier than his labour required. It was in his opinion that his life would be worth little if he could not spend an hour, or at least half an hour with his almighty God. So in silent prayer and meditation he would prepare for his daily work.

In the beautiful spring and summer mornings he would take Mary with him to a little arbour at the end of the garden, where, amid the songs of birds, they could sit and look upon the garden, rich with blossoms and sparkling with dew, and upon a far-reaching landscape bathed in the golden rays of the morning sun. Here he conversed with her about God, who causes the sun to shine, and sends the fertilizing rain and dew, who feeds the birds of the air and clothes the flowers of the field in such regal beauty. Here he taught her to know the Almighty God as the loving Father of all men. He told her about the Almighty Father who draws us to him and wins our love through his beloved and only begotten Son. Here Jacob taught his daughter to pray by kneeling with her and yielding up his soul in heart-felt prayer. This all contributed greatly towards planting in Mary's heart the seeds of piety and devotion.

Mary's favourite flowers were the violet, the lily and the rose. Jacob loved to point to them as emblems of the virtues most becoming to a woman. In early March when she brought the first violet to him and joyfully called upon to admire it, he said:

"Let the modest violet, my dear Mary, be to you an image of humility. Let it remind you of the benefits of doing good in secret. The violet clothes itself in the tender colours of modesty; it prefers to bloom in shaded, secret corners; it fills the air with its fragrance while remaining hidden beneath the leaves. May you also, my dear Mary, be like the retiring violet, avoiding vain display, not seeking to attract the public eye, but preferring to do good in quiet and peace."

One morning when the roses and lilies were in full bloom, and the garden appeared in its richest array, Jacob said to his daughter, as he pointed to a beautiful lily, which was beaming in the morning sun:

"Let the lily, my dear child, be to you the emblem of purity. Look how beautiful, how pure and fair it is! The whitest linen is as nothing compared with the purity of its petals; they are like the snow. Happy is the young woman whose heart is as pure and as free from stain! But the purest of all colours is also the hardest to preserve pure. The petal of the lily is easily soiled; touch it carelessly or roughly and a stain is left behind. In the same way a word, or a thought may stain the purity of innocence!"

Then pointing to a rose he said, "Let the rose, my dear Mary, be to you an emblem of modesty. More beautiful than the colour of the rose is the blush that rises to the cheek of a modest girl. It is a sign that she is still pure of heart and innocent of thought. Happy is the young girl who blushes at even the suggestion of a wrong or impure thought. This means that she is put on her guard against the approach of danger."

Jacob plucked several roses and lilies, tied them together in a bunch, and gave them to Mary, with the words:

"The lily and the rose, sister flowers as they are, belong one to the other. They are both incomparable in their beauty, they are made even more lovely by being together. In the same way, my dear child innocence and modesty cannot be separated. Yes, God designed that modesty should be the constant and faithful sister of innocence. Modesty preserves Innocence and protects it from danger. Remain modest, my beloved daughter, and you will also remain innocent. May your heart be ever pure like the snow-white lily, and your cheeks will ever resemble the rose in beauty."

Among the many fruit-trees that adorned the garden there was one that was prized above all the others. It was an apple-tree, not much larger than a rose-bush, and stood by itself in a bed in the middle of the garden. Mary's father had planted it on the day that she was born, and every year it bore a number of beautiful golden apples. Once it blossomed earlier than usual and with unusual luxuriance. The tree was one mass of blossom. Mary was so delighted with it that she went every morning as soon as she was dressed to look at it.

Once, when it was in full bloom, she called to her father and said:

"Look, Father, how beautiful! Was there ever such a lovely mingling of red and white! The whole tree looks like one huge bunch of flowers!"

The next morning she hastened into the garden to feast her eyes once more upon the tree. But what was her grief to see that the frost had nipped it and destroyed all its flowers. They had all become brown and yellow, and when the sun came forth in its strength they withered and fell to the ground. Mary wept bitter tears at the sight.

Mary's father turned to her and said: "This is how sinful pleasure destroys the bloom of youth. Always remember, Mary, how dreadful it is to be seduced from the right path! This apple tree is an example of what would happen if you were to wander from the way. Mary up to now your life shows much promise. If this promise was not fulfilled, if you wandered away from the right way, life would have no joys for me. With tears in my eyes I should go down sorrowfully to my grave!"

As he spoke tears pricked his eyes. Mary was deeply moved. His words made so profound an impression upon her she never forgot them.

Under the eyes of a loving and wise father, and amid the flowers of her garden, Mary grew daily in stature and intelligence - blooming as a rose, pure as a lily, modest and retiring as a violet, and as full of promise as a tree laden with blossom.

Jacob was always happy to see how his hard work was rewarded by the fruits of his garden. But his true happiness was when he looked upon the pious heart and mind of his beloved daughter!

Mary at the Castle

One lovely morning in the middle of May Mary had gone into a wood not far from the house to cut some sallows and twigs of hazel. These her father used to make pretty little baskets when the garden did not require his care. That morning she came upon a hollow covered with lilies of the valley. They were the first of the year, and in her delight she plucked enough to make two bunches - one for her father, and one for herself.

As she was making her way home through the meadows she was met by the Countess and her daughter Amelia, who generally resided in the capital, but who, a few days previously, had come to make a short stay at the castle of Terborg.

Mary, as soon as she saw the ladies, who

were dressed in white and carried green parasols, stepped politely to one side in order to allow them to pass, at the same time curtseying respectfully, as was the custom of the time.

"Oh, what lovely lilies of the valley! Are they already in bloom?" exclaimed the young Countess, who loved these flowers more than all the others.

On hearing these words Mary at once offered one of the bouquets to each of the ladies. They received them with pleasure, and the Countess, taking out a richly-embroidered silk purse, was about to give her money for them.

But Mary said: "Oh no, my lady, I cannot accept anything for my flowers. Pray permit a poor girl, whose father has received many kindnesses at the Count's hands, to have the pleasure of offering you this little gift without thinking of reward."

The Countess was pleased, and with a friendly smile said:

"If you will, you may from time to time bring a bunch of lilies to the castle for my daughter. She will be delighted to have them."

Mary promised to do so; and every morning, as long as the flowers lasted, she carried a bunch to the house.

So as it turned out Mary was often in contact with the young Countess Amelia. Daily Amelia grew more attached to Mary, greatly admiring her natural good sense, her unvarying cheerfulness, and her modest and retiring disposition. She was, in consequence, called upon to spend many an hour in Amelia's company long after the lilies of the valley had ceased to bloom. Indeed the young Countess made no secret of her desire to see Mary constantly with her, and even gave more than one hint that she would like to have her in her service.

Amelia's birthday now drew near, and Mary thought she would like to make her a little present. She had given her so many bouquets that a desire arose in her mind to take her something different.

During the foregoing winter Mary's father had employed his spare time making ladies' work-baskets, and one of the most beautiful of them all he had given to his daughter. He had seen the design for it in the city, and had put his very best work into it. Mary decided to fill this basket with the choicest flowers, and to give it to Amelia as a birthday present. Jacob willingly yielded his consent to this idea, and in order to further enhance the beauty and value of the gift he wove into the basket the letters of the young Countess's name and the crest of her family.

The expected day having arrived, early in the morning Mary gathered the freshest roses, the most beautiful white, crimson, and purple stocks, dark brown and yellow wallflowers, the richest pinks, and other flowers of the most exquisite colours. She plucked also some green branches full of foliage. She then displayed the flowers in the basket, intermingling them with the green leaves. The result was that all the colours, though perfectly distinct, were yet sweetly and delicately blended. One light garland, composed of rosebuds and moss, was passed round the basket, and the name of Amelia could be distinctly read enclosed in a coronet of forget-me-nots. The effect of the fresh rosebuds, the tender moss, and the blue forget-me-nots upon the white latticework of the basket was very beautiful. Indeed, so perfect did Mary's little present look as a whole, that the grave father praised her good taste with a contented smile, and said: "Let it stand there a little, so that I may have the pleasure of looking at it a while longer."

Mary then went to the castle with her present, which she offered to the Countess Amelia, adding the best wishes of her heart for her young friend's happiness. The young Countess was just then getting ready for her guests. Behind her stood her maid, dressing her hair for the birthday feast. Amelia received her present with pleasure. She could hardly find terms in which to express her delight as she viewed the charming flowers so tastefully arranged in the basket.

"Dear Mary," she said, "you have robbed your garden to make me so rich a present, and as to the basket, I have never seen anything like it in all my life. Come, let us go and show it to my mother."

She then took Mary in the most friendly manner by the hand, and led her upstairs to her mother's room.

"See, Mother!" exclaimed Amelia, as she entered the room, "what a lovely present Mary has brought me! Never have you seen so beautiful a basket, and where can one find such exquisite flowers?"

The Countess also was greatly pleased with the basket of flowers.

"In truth," she said, "this basket, with its flowers yet wet with dew, is really charming. It equals the most experienced efforts of the pencil. It does honour to Mary's taste, but more to the kindness of her heart. Wait a little, my child," she said to Mary, while she made a sign to Amelia to follow her into the adjoining room.

"Amelia," said the Countess, "Mary must not be permitted to go away without some suitable return. What do you think it will be best to give her?"

Amelia reflected for a moment, and then said: "I think that one of my dresses would be best. There is one dress that has flowers embroidered on it that is almost as good as new. I have worn it but once or twice. It is a little too short for me, but it will fit Mary exactly, and she can arrange it herself, she has so much taste. If it is not too much, I will give it to her."

"Do so," said the Countess. "When you give anything to those of humble means it ought always to be something serviceable. Your dress with the flowers will suit the little flower girl very well."

When they returned to the room in which they had left Mary, the Countess said: "Go now, my children, and take good care of the flowers, lest they fade before dinner. I want the guests to admire the basket also, which will be the most beautiful ornament on the table. As to you, dear Mary, I will leave Amelia to thank you for your present."

Amelia ran to her room with Mary, and told her maid to bring the robe. Juliette (for that was her name) stood looking at her, and said: "Your ladyship cannot surely intend to wear that dress today?"

"No," replied Amelia, "I wish to make a present of it to Mary."

"Give that dress away!" exclaimed Juliette. "Does her ladyship, your mother, know that?"

"Bring me the robe," said Amelia decidely. "Leave the rest to me."

Juliette turned her face to hide her vexation, and went away, her face burning with anger. She opened the wardrobe with a pull, and took out the dress.

"Oh, if I only dared to tear it to pieces!" she exclaimed. "This gardener's girl has won some of the favour of my young mistress from me, and now she steals from me this dress, for it belongs by right to me when my mistress has done with it. I could tear the eyes out of this hateful flower girl. But I will be revenged."

Suppressing her anger, however, she

returned with a pleasant smile to the room, and gave the dress to Amelia.

"Dear Mary," said Amelia, "I have had presents to-day much more valuable than your basket, but none which gives me so much pleasure. The flowers in this robe are not nearly so beautiful as yours, but I think, out of love for me, you will not despise them. Wear it for my sake; and give my kindest wishes to your father."

Mary took the dress, kissed the hand of the young Countess, and hastened home, her heart full of joy.

Juliette, jealous and enraged, continued her work in silence. It cost her many a struggle before she could finish dressing her young mistress's hair, but she could not totally dissemble her wrath.

"Are you angry, Juliette?" asked the young Countess.

"I should be very silly," answered Juliette, "were I to be angry because your ladyship chooses to be generous."

"That is a very sensible speech," rejoined Amelia. "I hope you will always feel as reasonable."

When she reached her father's cottage, Mary was all eagerness to tell her good fortune. But Jacob was too prudent a man to take much pleasure in so rich a present. He shook his grey head, and said: "I would rather you had not carried the basket to the castle, but it cannot be helped now. This dress is truly valuable as a present from those whom we so highly respect. But I fear it will rouse the envy of others, and, what is still worse, that it will fill your own heart with vanity. Take care, my dear child, that the latter, at least, does not befall you. Modesty and good behaviour are more becoming in a young girl than the most beautiful and costly garments. Remember the Bible says it is 'the ornament of a meek and quiet spirit' which in the sight of God is of great price."

The Lost Ring

Scarcely had Mary had time to try on her beautiful dress, fold it up and put it away in her box, when the young Countess, pale, trembling, and almost out of breath, hastily entered the little cottage. Mary wondered what could be the matter; but before she had time to speak, Amelia exclaimed: "Oh, Mary, what have you done? My mother's diamond ring is missing, and no one was in the chamber but you. Oh, give it to me, quickly, or there will be a terrible to-do! Give it to me quickly, and then nothing more need be said."

Mary, as may well be imagined, became exceedingly frightened, and turned pale as death. "Oh, my lady," she exclaimed, "what can this mean? I have not got the ring! I did not even see a ring in the room; nor

29

did I move from the place where I stood."

But all her declarations could not convince Amelia, who continued to urge her to give up the ring.

"Mary," she pleaded, "I entreat you for your own sake to give me the ring. You know not how valuable and precious is the one stone it contains. The ring cost nearly a thousand silver coins. If you had known that, I am sure you would not have taken it. You thought it only a trifle of little value. Give it to me, I beseech you, and all shall be forgiven you as an act of youthful folly."

Mary wept bitterly at this suspicion. "Truly," she said, "I know nothing about the ring. I have never ventured to touch that which did not belong to me, much less to steal it. My dear father has taught me too well for me to do a thing of that kind."

At this moment the old man came in. He was at work in the garden when he saw the young Countess enter in such haste, and he returned to the house to see what was the matter; and when he was told he was so utterly overcome that he was obliged to seize hold of the corner of a table and sink upon a bench. When he could command himself sufficiently to speak, he said: "My dear child, to steal a ring of this value is a crime which, in this country, is punished with death. But this is only the part of the matter the least to be considered. Remember the command of God, 'Thou shalt not steal'. This action not only renders you responsible to men, but to that God who reads the heart, and with whom all false denials amount to nothing. Have you forgotten the holy commandment of God? Have you forgotten my fatherly advice? Did you allow yourself to be dazzled, and so to be led away by the splendour of the gold and the precious stone? If so, do not deny the fact, but restore the ring. That is the only way in which you can make good your fault, so far as it is possible to make it good."

"Oh, Father," said Mary, sobbing bitterly, "I assure you I have seen nothing of the ring. If I had even found such a ring in the street, I could not have rested till I restored it to its owner. Indeed, I have it not."

"See," the father continued, "this angel, the young Countess, who has come here out of love for you, to save you from the hands of justice; who means so well with you, who has just given you so valuable a present. She does not deserve that you should tell her a lie. If you have the ring say so at once, and the gracious young Countess will, by her intercession, save you from the punishment you deserve. Mary, I entreat you to be honest and speak the truth!"

"Father," said Mary, "you well know that I never in my life stole anything, even of so small a value as a farthing. I have never even ventured to take an apple from a tree or a handful of grass from the meadow of another. How could I take anything so valuable? Oh, believe me, Father, for I never in my life have told you a lie."

"Mary," again said her father, "see my grey hairs. Oh! do not bring them down with sorrow to the grave. Spare me so great an affliction. Tell me, before God, before whom I hope soon to appear, in whose kingdom there is no place for unrepentant thieves - tell me if you have the ring. For your soul's sake I implore you to tell the truth!"

Mary raised her eyes, which were filled with tears, to heaven, and said in the most solemn manner: "God knows I have not the ring! As surely as I hope for salvation, so surely I have it not!"

Convinced now of the innocence of his daughter, the old man said: "I do believe you have not the ring. You would not dare to lie in the presence of God, and here before the young Countess and myself. And since I now believe you to be innocent, I am easy. Be you also at peace, my child, and fear nothing. There is but one real evil in the world that we need fear, and that is sin. Prison and death are as nothing to it. Whatever may become of us, even if all men should forsake us and turn against us, we should still have God for our friend, and he will certainly rescue us, and sooner or later bring our innocence to light. Remember what he says: 'I will make thy righteousness as clear as the light, and thy just dealings as the noonday."

The young Countess wiped away a tear as she said: "When I hear you speak in this way, I also believe that you have not got the ring. But when I examine all the circumstances, no other explanation seems possible. My mother remembers distinctly the very place on her work-table where she put it down before I went into the room with Mary. Not a living soul was there but her. That I did not go near the work-table Mary herself can vouch. While Mother and I were speaking together in the next room Mary was left alone; before and after her no one went into the room. After we had gone Mother closed the door in order to change her dress. When she had finished dressing, and wished to put on her ring, it was missing. Mother herself carefully searched the room for it. She took the precaution to allow no one, not even me, to enter the room until she had examined it thoroughly two or three times. But all in vain. Who then can have taken it?"

"That is impossible for me to say," replied Jacob. "May God support us in this severe trial. But whatever may be hanging over us," he said, looking up to heaven, "behold, Lord, I am ready. Give me thy grace, O God! That will suffice."

"I return to the castle with a heavy heart," said the young Countess. "Was there ever so sad a birthday? And I see no end of the trouble to come out of it. My mother as yet has spoken to no one on the subject but myself; but it will not be possible to keep the secret. She must wear the ring today. My father, whom we expect from court at noon, will immediately notice if she is without it. He gave it to her the day that I was born; and she has never ceased to wear it on each succeeding anniversary. She fully believes that I shall take it back with me. "Farewell," continued Amelia, after a pause. "I will say that I consider you to be innocent; but who will believe?"

She went out overwhelmed with sadness, and her eyes filled with tears. Father and daughter were so overcome with grief that they could not even accompany her to the door.

Jacob seated himself upon a bench, resting his head on his hand, with his eyes fixed on the earth. The tears chased themselves down his wrinkled cheeks. Mary threw herself at his knees, and said: "Oh, father! Indeed I am innocent of this affair, indeed I am!"

He raised her up, looked long and earnestly into her eyes, and then said: "Yes Mary, you are innocent. Guilt could never wear so honest and truthful a look."

"Oh, Father," Mary added, "what will be the end of all this? What will become of us? If it were I alone who was to suffer, I could bear it; but that you, my dear father, should suffer on my account - that gives me more pain that all the rest."

"Trust in God," answered her father, "and be not dismayed. Without his permission not a hair of our heads can be touched. Whatever may befall us it is all ordered by God. It is all therefore for the best, and for our good. What more can we want? Have no fear, then, but always keep strictly to the truth. However you may be threatened, or what promise may be held out to you, do not depart a hair's-breadth from truth. A clear conscience is a good pillow even in a dungeon. We may expect to be separated. Your father, my dear child, will no longer be with you to console you. But do not let that trouble you; cling all the closer to your Father which is in heaven. He is a powerful protector of innocence, and nothing can deprive you of his support."

While they were thus speaking the door was thrown open, and the officers of justice entered the room. Mary uttered a cry, and fell into the arms of her father.

"Separate them!" cried the chief officer, his eyes gleaming with wrath. "Put the daughter in irons and take her to prison. Let the father also be held in safe keeping." He then ordered that the house and garden should be carefully guarded, and that no one should be allowed to enter until he and the sheriff had had them thoroughly searched.

The officers seized Mary, who clung to her father with her all might, but they tore her from the arms of the old man and put her in irons. She fainted, and in that state was carried away. When father and daughter were taken into the street a great crowd had already gathered. The story of the ring had spread like wildfire through the whole village; everybody in the place seemed to have collected round the little cottage, and the most conflicting opinions were expressed as to what had taken place. Notwithstanding the kindness Mary and her father had shown towards them all, there were many who were pleased to see them in trouble, and who put the worst construction on what had happened. The comfort which Jacob and Mary had acquired by their hard work had given rise to much envy.

"Now," said some, "we know where all these good things came from; we were never quite able to understand it before. If this be the method, it is no great merit to live in abundance, and be better clad than other people."

Nevertheless, the inhabitants of Terborg, for the most part, showed compassion for Jacob and his daughter in their trouble, and many a father and mother were heard to say: "Even the best of us are liable to fall. Who would have believed this of these good people? But perhaps it is not as is thought. If so, may God bring their innocence to light! And even if they are guilty, may God be with them and incline their hearts to confess their sin and to amend, and thus escape the great misery that threatens them! May he in his mercy guard us all from sin, for without his help we are not safe for a single day."

Many of the children of the village were gathered together with the rest, and when Mary and her father passed, they cried and said: "Ah, if they are put in prison there will be no kind Jacob to give us fruit, nor Mary to make us presents of flowers. They ought not to do it."

Mary in Prison

Mary was almost insensible when they took her to prison. When she recovered from her swoon, she wept, sobbed and wrung her hands. Then remembering where alone comfort was to be found, she prayed. At length, overcome with terror, overwhelmed with sadness, and exhausted from having shed so many tears, she threw herself upon her bed of straw, and a sweet sleep soon closed her heavy eyelids. When she awoke, it was already night, and the darkness prevented her from distinguishing a single object. It was a long while before she knew where she was. The story of the ring appeared to her as a dream, and at first she thought herself on her own little bed; she was consoling herself with that idea when she felt the irons upon her hands.

Frightened by the noise of the chains, she sprang up from her bed of straw, and all the sad reality burst upon her mind.

"Oh, what can I do!" she cried, falling on her knees, "O gracious God! Look down into this dismal prison and see me on my knees before thee! Thou knowest that I am innocent! Thou art the only help of the innocent! Save me! Have compassion upon me, and on my poor father! Give him some comfort, even if I must feel a double share of sorrow!"

The recollection of her father caused a torrent of tears to flow from her eyes. She continued for a long time to cry and sob.

The moon, which had until then been covered by large clouds, now shone in full splendour, and threw on the floor of the cell the shadow of the barred window. Mary could easily distinguish the four walls of her narrow prison; the rough stones of which they were constructed; the white lines of mortar where the stones were joined together; the little projection in the wall which served in place of a table; the earthen pitcher and small bowl that stood upon it; and the bundle of straw for a bed. But despite her misery, Mary felt comforted. The bright moon seemed like an old friend.

"Do you come, lovely moon," she said, "to look in at me as upon an old friend? Oh, when you shone into my little room at home, how much more beautiful you seemed than now, through the iron grating of a prison! Are you sad for me? Ah, how little I thought I should ever see you in such a position! Do you look down also upon my dear father? What is he doing? Is he awake, and watching you in sorrow, as I am? Oh that I might see him for a moment, as you do! Could you but speak, O lovely moon! You might tell him how Mary is weeping and mourning for him." The poor broken-hearted girl was silent for a moment. Then she said: "Oh, how foolishly I have been speaking in my sorrow! Forgive me God for these idle words, O most gracious Father - you see where my father lies! You see him and me! You see into both our hearts! Your help is not hindered by prison walls and iron bars! Send comfort to my beloved father in his trouble."

Mary then noticed with astonishment that the cell was pervaded by a sweet perfume. She had in the morning tied together a few half-opened rosebuds and other flowers that were left over from the birthday basket, making of them a little posy which she pinned to her breast. The perfume came from these flowers.

"Are you still there, dear flowers?" she said, as she caught sight of the posy. "And must you also come with me to prison, you innocent creatures? What have you done to deserve punishment? Ah, sweet friends in sorrow, there is my comfort - that I have merited this punishment as little as you!"

She took the little bouquet from her breast, and looked at it by the light of the moon. "Ah!" she exclaimed, "when I gathered these rosebuds this morning in my garden, and plucked these forget-me-nots by the side of the brook, who would have thought that I should in the evening be lying in this prison? When I fastened the garland of flowers round the edge of the basket, who would have imagined that tonight iron fetters would be fastened round my wrists? So uncertain are all things on earth. No one knows how soon their position may be changed, and to what sad events his most innocent actions may lead! We must, every morning, ask God for his protection!"

Again she wept. The tears fell upon the rosebuds and forget-me-nots, and glittered in the moonlight like dew. "He who forgets not the flowers, but refreshes them with rain and dew," she said, "will not forget me. Oh, most merciful God, send comfort into my heart, and into the heart of my dear father, as you fill the cups of the thirsty flowers with the dews of heaven!"

Amid her tears she again thought of her father. "Oh, my good and kind father," she said, "when I look at this little bouquet, how many of your wise words about the flowers come back to my recollection!

"This rosebud grew amid thorns, so may joy spring out of my sorrows. Whoever had tried to unfold this rosebud before its time would have destroyed it. God, who created it, has ordained that its tender petals should open gently bit by bit, and should breathe forth their delightful perfume. Thus will he turn my sufferings to account, so that the blessings they are intended to develop may come forth. Therefore will I patiently wait until his appointed time.

"These forget-me-nots remind me of their Creator. My gracious God, I will not forget you, as you have not forgotten me! They are blue, these flowers, like the heavens above; and in heaven is my comfort amidst all the world's trials and sorrows.

"Here is a sweet-smelling sweet-pea, with its delicate red and white blossom! This slender plant climbs up the staff, without it it would be creeping in the dust. As this plant clings to the staff so I will cling to God, and rise above the stains and griefs of life!

"This mignonette more than all the other flowers diffuses its delicious fragrance through the cell. Sweet, gentle flower, even though I plucked you, you delight me with your perfume. I will strive to be like you - little flower. I will endeavour to feel kindly towards those who have torn me from my garden and cast me into this prison, although I did them no harm.

"Here is a sprig of periwinkle. It shows its fresh bright leaves even in winter, and in the most dreary days of the year gladdens us with the colour of hope. I will hope! Even in this hour of deepest suffering I will not give up hope. God preserves this little plant fresh and green amid the storms of winter, and amid ice and snow. God will also preserve me - amid the storms of misfortune.

"The flowers of earth do not last for

long. Like so many joys and pleasures of life they soon wither and fade away. But in heaven above, after the brief sorrows of earth, there awaits a blessedness and a glory which is everlasting and fadeth not away!"

A dark cloud now suddenly obscured the moon. Mary could no longer see her flowers, and a darkness that could almost be felt filled her cell. Once more her heart sank within her. But the cloud soon passed away, and the moon again shone as brightly as before. Mary sighed, "Innocence for a time may be under a cloud, but in the end it shines forth again in all its brightness and beauty. In the same way, O God, help my innocence to triumph over all false accusations."

Comforted and encouraged by these reflections, Mary bowed herself in prayer, and then laid herself down upon her bundle of straw and fell into a peaceful sleep. A pleasant dream came to her in her slumbers, and soothed and calmed her still more. She thought she was wandering in the moonlight in a strange garden, situated in the midst of a rough wilderness full of gloomy fir-trees. But the garden had a rare loveliness and charm. Never had she seen

the moon so bright and beautiful. All the
flowers in the garden seemed to become
more beautiful in its soft and tender light.
Her father also appeared to her in the
entrancing garden. The moonbeams
lighted his face, which was now smiling
and happy. She ran to him, and, throwing
her arms about his neck, shed tears of joy,
with which her cheeks were still wet when
she awoke.

The Trial

Mary was scarcely awake when an officer came to take her to the tribunal. She trembled at the sight of the dark court room. The judge was seated on a chair covered with scarlet. The clerk stood by an enormous black table, filled with writings. The judge asked Mary some questions, and she answered them, truthfully. She sobbed and wept, but still declared her innocence.

"Do not attempt to make me believe what is impossible," said the judge. "No one but yourself entered the room - no one but you, then, can have the ring. You had better confess, therefore, that you have it at once."

"I cannot," Mary answered, weeping; "I cannot speak anything but the truth. I know nothing whatever of the ring. I have not seen it, and I have not got it."

"The ring was seen in your hands," continued the judge. "Will you deny that?"

Mary persisted that the thing was impossible. The judge then rang a little bell, and Juliette was brought in.

Juliette, in the fit of jealousy which the dress given to Mary had caused, and in the guilty design of depriving her of the favour of her mistress, had said to the people of the castle: "No one else has the ring but that detestable girl, the gardener's daughter. When she was coming downstairs I saw her looking at a ring set with precious stones which she had in her hand. She was startled when she saw me, and put it out of sight. Her action struck me as being very suspicious. However, I did not wish to be hasty and so said nothing. Perhaps, thought I, they have given her the ring as they have given her so many other things. If she had stolen it, I knew it would soon be missed, and then it would be time enough to speak. I am very glad that I had no occasion to go into the Countess's room. Such wicked people as that hypocritical girl might cause suspicion to fall on others, more honest than them."

As a result of all these falsehoods,

Juliette was summoned as a witness, and lest she should be caught in a lie, she determined to maintain it, even in a court of justice. When she was summoned, and the judge required her to declare the truth before God, she felt her heart beat quickly, and her knees trembled under her. But the wicked girl listened neither to the voice of the judge, nor to that of her own conscience. "If," she said to herself, "I acknowledge now that I have lied, then I shall be driven away, or perhaps imprisoned." She persisted in her lie, therefore, and, addressing herself to Mary, she said with effrontery, "You have the ring; I saw you with it."

Mary heard this with horror, but she did not allow her emotions to get the better of her judgment. She could not, however, refrain from weeping. She almost choked on her tears. "It is not true. You did not see me with the ring. How can you say such a wicked lie? How can you bring misery upon me? I have never done you any harm."

But Juliette, who only thought of herself, and felt nothing but hatred and jealousy towards Mary, persisted in her accusation. She repeated the lie with additional circumstances and details, and then was dismissed by the judge.

"You are convicted," said the judge to Mary. "Every circumstance is against you. Moreover, the chamber-maid of the young Countess saw the ring in your hands. Tell me now what you have done with it."

Mary still asserted that she had it not. Then, in accordance with the cruel custom of those days, the judge had Mary whipped. She screamed with the pain and wept. Praying to God for his support, Mary continued to repeat that she was innocent, but it was all in vain.

Pale, trembling she was again thrown into prison. Her wounds gave her great pain. Stretched on a bed of straw extremely hard, she passed half the night without sleep. She wept, groaned, and prayed to God, who at last sent her a sweet and soothing sleep.

The next day the judge had her brought again before his tribunal. As severity had answered no purpose, he endeavoured to draw from her an acknowledgment by mildness and flattering promises.

"You have incurred the penalty of death; but confess where the ring is, and nothing more shall be done to you. The whipping you have received shall be your punishment. You shall return peaceably to your home with your father. Consider well, and choose - it is between life and death! I wish to be lenient with you. What good will the stolen ring be to you if you are dead?"

Still Mary stood firm to her first assertion.

The judge, who had remarked how much she loved her father, continued: "If you persist in concealing the truth - if you will not spare your own life, spare at least that of your aged father. Would you see your father killed by the hand of the executioner? Who but he could have induced you to tell a falsehood with so much obstinacy? Are you ignorant that his life as well as yours is at stake?"

So terrified was Mary at these words that she nearly fainted.

"Confess," said the judge, "that you have taken the ring. A single word, the simple syllable 'yes', and you save your life and that of your father."

The temptation was great, and for sometime Mary was silent. It was a moment of dreadful trial. The thought came into her mind that she might say, "I took the ring, but I lost it on the road." But "No," she thought afterwards; "no it is better to keep to the truth. It is a sin to lie. Let it cost me what it will, I will not depart from the truth, even to save my own and my father's life. I will obey God, and leave it all in his hand. I am confident in his goodness and might."

She then answered in a determined but trembling voice, "If I were to say I had the ring, it would be a lie, and though this falsehood should save my life, I would not utter it. But" Mary continued, "if blood must be shed, spare my dear father! For him I shall be most happy to shed my blood."

These words touched the hearts of all those who were present. The judge himself, with all his severity, could not help being moved. He remained silent, and made a sign for Mary to be conducted back to prison.

A Mournful Interview

The judge had great difficulty in coming to a decision. "Today is the third day," he said, "and we are no farther than the first hour. If there was any possibility that the ring was in other hands, I would believe the girl innocent. Such obstinacy at so tender an age is unheard of. But all the circumstances are too clearly against her. It is impossible that it can be otherwise; she must have stolen the ring."

He returned to the Countess, and again questioned her as to the most minute circumstances; Juliette was also re-examined. He passed the whole day in reviewing the testimony, and weighing each word that Mary had uttered in her examination. At length, very late in the evening he sent to the prison for Mary's father to be brought to his house.

"Jacob," he began, "I am known to be a severe man. However, no one can accuse me of ever intentionally injuring anyone. You will believe, I hope, that I do not desire the death of your daughter; nevertheless, all the circumstances prove that she must have committed the theft, and the law requires that she must die. The testimony of the chamber-maid puts the question beyond doubt. If, however, the ring were returned, and the damage repaired, we might grant her a pardon in consideration of her youth. But if she persists so obstinately in her guilty lies, it must be because, though young in years, she is old in wickedness. Then there is nothing to save her from death. Go to her, persuade her to return the ring, and I pledge my word that then, and only then, she shall not suffer the penalty of death. She shall be let off with a less severe punishment. You are her father, and have great influence over her. If you cannot induce her to acknowledge her guilt, what can we think except that you are her accomplice, and have participated in the crime? I repeat, if the ring be not produced, I shall show no mercy."

"I will speak to my daughter," Jacob

answered, "but that she has not stolen the ring, and therefore cannot acknowledge herself guilty, I know beforehand. I will, however, do all in my power. If she must die, despite her innocence, it is a great mercy to be permitted to see her once more."

An officer was sent with the old man to Mary's cell; he set the lamp on the little stone table. The officer then left the cell, closed the door, and left father and daughter alone together.

Mary was lying on her straw bed, her face turned to the wall, in a quiet doze. Just then though she opened her eyes and noticed the pale light of the lamp. She turned over and saw her father. With a cry of joy she sprang to her feet so hastily that it caused her chains to clang on the stone floor. Nearly fainting, Mary threw herself on her father. The old man sat down with her upon the bed, and pressed her in his arms; both remained for some time silent, and mingled their tears together.

Jacob then broke the silence, and began to speak as his commission required.

"Father," said Mary, interrupting him, "you cannot doubt my innocence. Is there no one who does not think me guilty - no one, not even my father? Believe me - your daughter is not a thief."

"Be calm, dear child - I believe you. What I have done is in compliance with the order I received."

Both again were silent. Jacob looked at Mary, and saw her cheeks pale and hollow with grief, her eyes red and swollen with weeping, and her long fair hair flowing dishevelled about her shoulders. "Poor child," he said, "God has given you a severe trial; but I fear that the most cruel, the most dreadful is yet to come. You, my child, may have to die by the hand of the executioner."

Mary replied, "I care but little for myself. God grant that I may not have the added sorrow of seeing you suffer such a death!"

"Fear not for me, dear child," said Jacob "I am in no danger. But you are in great danger. I hope for the best, but fear there is little chance of your life being spared."

"Oh," cried Mary, transported with joy, and without allowing her father time to finish, "if this is the case, my heart is relieved of a great weight. All is well! Be assured, my father, that I do not fear death. I shall go to God, my Saviour, and I shall see my mother also in heaven. Oh, what a happiness that will be!"

These words made a deep impression on the heart of the old man, and he wept like a child. "Well, God be praised," said he, clasping his hands - "God be praised for the submissive disposition I find you in. It is hard, very hard, for an old man, for a tender father to lose his only child, his last support, and the joy of his old age. But," he continued in a broken voice, "Lord, thy will be done. Thou requirest a heavy sacrifice from a father's heart. But I bring it willingly. Take her to thyself. Into thy hands I commit her - my dearest on earth. To the everlasting care of your loving, fatherly, heart I commend her. In your keeping she will be safest. Ah, Mary, it is better that you die innocent, even by the hands of the executioner, than that I should live to see you robbed of your innocence, and fall into sin. Forgive me, my dear child, for speaking like this. You are very good while the world is wicked. It is even possible that you could fall into a life of sin. If it be God's will, then, that you should die be of good comfort. You die innocent, and that is the best way to die, even though it may be a violent death. You will be transplanted, like a pure white lily, from this rough world to your everlasting home in heaven!"

A torrent of tears for a time prevented Jacob from speaking. But after a while he said: "Yet one word more, my dear Mary. Juliette is the one whose evidence has condemned you. She declared on her oath that she saw you with the ring in your hand. On her testimony you die, if you are to die. But you pardon her, do you not? You will carry with you no feeling of hatred towards her? Even in this dark prison, on this hard bed, loaded with irons, you are happier than she is in the palace of her master, clothed with silk and lace, and surrounded with every luxury. It is better to die innocent than to live dishonoured. Do you pardon her, Mary, as your Saviour pardoned his enemies?"

Mary assured him that she did.

"Now," her father said, who heard the officer coming to separate them, "I commend you to God and his grace; and if you are not to see me again - if this is the last time I am allowed to speak with you, my daughter, at least I shall not be long in following you to heaven. I feel that I cannot long survive this parting."

The officer warned the old man that it was time to go. Mary wished to detain him, and held him in her arms with all her strength; but her father was obliged to disengage himself as gently as he could, and Mary fell insensible on her bed.

Jacob was again brought before the judge. As soon as he entered he raised his hands to heaven and cried out, almost beside himself, "My child is innocent - she is no thief. Before God I affirm it!"

"I would that I could believe so too," said the judge; "but unfortunately I cannot be guided by the protestations of yourself and your daughter; I must pronounce sentence according to the nature of the testimony, and as is prescribed by the letter of the law."

The Sentence and its Execution

As may well be imagined, all were curious to know what would be the outcome of this unfortunate affair in which Mary was involved. Friends and neighbours trembled for her life; for at this time the crime of theft was punished with great vigour - the death penalty. The Count wished that Mary should be found innocent. He read all the testimony, and had many consultations with the judge, without being able to convince himself of her innocence. It seemed almost impossible that anyone else could have the ring. The Countesses, mother and daughter, begged with tears in their eyes that Mary should not suffer death; while her aged father, in his cell, spent days and nights pleading with God that he would show the world the innocence of his daughter.

Whenever Mary heard the jailer approach with his clanking keys, she thought that he was coming to announce her death sentence. Meanwhile the executioner was engaged in preparing the place of execution, clearing away the weeds with which it had become overgrown.

Juliette, when out walking one day, saw him engaged in this work, and she felt a sudden pain in her heart, as though it had been pierced with a dagger. Horror seemed to deprive her of her presence of mind; and when she sat down to supper she could touch nothing. Pale and miserable looking everyone saw she was not in her ordinary spirits. She went to bed, but her sleep was disturbed. Her remorse gave her no rest either day or night; but the heart of the wicked creature was too hardened to confess her lies and, by saving Mary's life, atone in some measure for the evil she had done.

At length the judge pronounced sentence. Mary, on account of her theft, and her obstinate denial of it, was pronounced deserving of death, but in consideration of her extreme youth, and her hitherto unblemished reputation, the sentence of death was commuted to that of imprisonment for life in a house of correction. Her father, who was considered to be participator in her guilt, either as an actual accomplice, or through the evil training he had given her, was banished for ever from the province.

Their possessions were to be sold to contribute as far as they would go to the reparation of the loss which the Count had sustained, and to pay the expenses of the court.

The Count reduced the sentence further in that, instead of being sent to the house of correction, Mary was allowed to accompany her father into exile. It was also decided that, in order to spare their feelings as much as possible, they should be conducted across the frontier at daybreak the following morning before people were astir.

As Mary and her father passed before the castle gate, conducted by an officer of the jail, Juliette came out. Seeing that the affair, contrary to all expectation, had taken a different turn from what she anticipated, the heartless girl, destitute of every good sentiment, regained her gaiety. It had seemed to her too hard that Mary should lose her life, but she did not care about seeing her driven into exile through her wickedness. That, indeed, was just what she wanted. She had always feared that Mary would replace her. This fear was now dissipated. Her first aversion against Jacob's daughter revived, and she rejoiced at Mary's misfortune.

A few days before, the Countess, seeing Mary's basket upon the sideboard, had said to Juliette: "Take that basket away. It brings to my mind recollections so painful that I cannot see it without distress."

Juliette had taken it to her room, and now brought it out with her.

"Here," she cried, as Mary and her father approached; "here, take your fine present. My lady wishes to have nothing from such people as you. Your glory has passed away with your flowers, for which you were so well paid, and it is a great pleasure for me to give you back your basket."

She threw the basket at Mary's feet, re-entered the castle with a scornful laugh, and shut the gate with great violence behind her.

Mary took up the basket in silence, and with tears in her eyes, went on her way. Her father had not even a stick to help him on his journey. Mary had nothing but the basket. She turned to look back at her home more than a hundred times, her eyes wet with tears. After some time even the castle, and the steeple of the church were hidden by a hill covered with trees.

When the officer had conducted them to the stone marking the boundary of the province, which was deep in the forest, the old man, overwhelmed with anxiety and grief, seated himself upon the stone, which was covered with moss and shaded by an aged oak.

"Come, my daughter," said he; and as he took Mary in his arms, joined her hands in his, and raising them to heaven, said: "Before we go further let us thank God that he has brought us out of the dark, narrow prison into the free air and into the sight of the beautiful sky. He has saved our lives, and has restored you to my arms, my dearly beloved child."

Jacob raised his eyes to heaven, which could be seen clear and blue through the leaves of the old oak, and he prayed with a loud voice:

"Gracious Father in heaven! You are our only comfort! You are the almighty protector of all the oppressed! Accept our thanks for our release from prison and death. Receive our thanks for all the benefits you gave us in this place that we are now leaving. As we take this last look at our home we look to thee with grateful hearts. Before we go to this strange land we ask for your blessing. Look down on a poor father and his weeping child. Protect us and be our guide along the paths that we may yet have to tread. Lead us among good people, and incline their hearts to have compassion upon us. Let us once more find a little home to call our own. I believe that you have already prepared such a place for us. In this belief, and with perfect confidence in thee, we go on our way strengthened and comforted."

Mary repeated in her heart all her father's words. Both their hearts were filled with unspeakable joy, and with a courage glad and uplifting.

A Gleam of Sunshine

Mary and her father wandered on, day after day, until they were more than eighty miles from Terborg. During all that time, though they had tried hard, they had found no place to stay or where they could work to earn a living. The little money which they had was nearly exhausted, and they did not know what to do. At length they were reduced to begging. They knocked on a great number of doors, but were met with rejection often accompanied by abuse. Sometimes they were given a small piece of dry bread, which with some water from the nearest stream constituted their meal. Now and again they received a little soup or some cold vegetables, and now and again some remains of broken meat or pastry. For many days they would have nothing warm to eat, and at night they were glad to be able to find shelter in a barn.

One day when the road along which they travelled led between hills and mountains covered with trees, and they had walked for a long time without seeing any village, the old man was taken ill, very suddenly. He sank down, pale and speechless on a heap of dried leaves. Mary was nearly overcome with anguish and terror. In vain she sought for a little fresh water; not a single drop could she find. In vain she called aloud for assistance - the only voice she heard in reply was the sound of her own echo. On whatever side she looked no house was to be seen. Although almost worn out with fatigue, she climbed to the top of the hill, to get a better view of the surrounding country. Then she discovered, on the opposite side of the hill, a farm-house surrounded by ripening cornfields and green meadows, and completely shut in by the forest.

She ran down as fast as she could, and at length reached the house quite out of breath. With tears in her eyes, and a voice broken with sobs, she asked for help. Both the farmer and his wife, who were somewhat advanced in years, were good, kind-hearted people, and were deeply touched at the sight of the poor girl - her pale face, her tears, and the evident anguish of heart.

"Put a horse to the little wagon," said the farmer's wife to her husband, "and let us bring the sick old man here."

While the farmer went out to harness his horse and bring out his cart, his wife got ready a couple of eider-down beds, an earthen pitcher of fresh water, and a bottle of vinegar.

When Mary heard that the vehicle would be obliged to go round the hill, and that it was a good half-hour's drive, she hastened with the water and vinegar by the same path by which she had come, and by this means was soon at her father's side.

She found that he had recovered a little. He was sitting at the foot on a pine-tree, and was greatly rejoiced to see his daughter, whose absence had caused him some anxiety.

As soon as the farmer and his wife arrived they placed him in the wagon and conveyed him to the farm, where they gave him a neat little back room, with another room adjoining, and a kitchen, which were then unoccupied. The farmer's wife made him up a comfortable, nice bed. Mary was contented to lie in the couch in order to be near her father, so that he should want for nothing. Jacob's illness was the result of bad food, lack of rest, and a tiring journey.

The good farmer's wife withheld nothing that the house contained that could in any way refresh and restore the poor old man. She spared neither meal nor eggs, milk nor butter; even a few chickens were gladly sacrificed to make nourishing soup for the weak old man. Nor was that all, for after a day or two the farmer took to bringing in a young pigeon from time to time.

"There!" he would say to his wife, with a smile. "Cook that for him. As you do not spare the poultry, I must do something too."

These kind people had been in the habit of going every year to a fair in the neighbouring village, but they agreed this time to remain at home, and to use the money which they would have spent at the fair in buying medicines and delicacies for the invalid instead. Mary thanked them with tears in her eyes. She thanked God, too, for bringing them to such kind and hospitable people. "Praise God," she said, "there are kind people everywhere, and it is often in the most unlikely places that we find the most compassionate hearts."

Mary was constantly seated beside her father's bed ready to attend to his smallest want; but she did not sit there idle. She was skilled at knitting and sewing, and busily occupied herself for the farmer's household. She did not give herself a moment's rest. The farmer's wife was greatly pleased with her work, and her modest and reserved demeanour.

By the great care which they had taken of Jacob, and by the excellent food which they had given him, he was soon able to sit up; and, as idleness had never been in his nature, he began again to resume his basket-making. Mary, as before, gathered for him branches of willow and hazel twigs, and his first production was a pretty little convenient basket, which he offered to the farmer's wife as a token of gratitude.

He had exactly guessed her taste. The basket was elegant, but strong and solid; branches of willow, stained with deep red, and interwoven in the cover, formed the initials of the farmer's wife, and the year in which the basket was made. The border was formed of green, brown, and yellow reeds, representing a cottage thatched with straw, on each side of which was a pine-tree. This pretty basket was the admiration of the whole house. The farmer's wife received the present with great joy. She was also delighted that Jacob had included pine trees in the basket as the farm was actually called "Pine Farm". When Jacob had recovered, he said to his hosts: "We have been a burden long enough. It is time I should go and seek my fortune elsewhere."

"What is the matter with you, my good Jacob?" said the farmer, taking him by the hand. "I hope we have not offended you. You are a sensible man why should you wish to leave us?"

The farmer's wife was deeply moved, and as she wiped the tears from her eyes, she said: "Why not remain where you are? The year is already far advanced. Look at the leaves on the trees. Winter is almost already at our doors. Do you wish to be sick again?"

Jacob assured them he had no other motive for leaving them than the fear of being troublesome.

"Troublesome!" exclaimed the farmer;

"don't distress yourself on that account. In the little room there you are in nobody's way, and you earn enough to supply all your wants."

"Yes, indeed," added the farmer's wife; "Mary alone earns enough with her needle and her knitting; and if you, Jacob, are inclined to go on with your basket-making, you will find enough to do. Not many days since, when I went to the christening of the miller's child, I took your pretty basket with me. All the women who were there admired it and wished to have one like it. I will undertake to get you plenty of orders, if you like. You won't lack for work, I assure you."

Jacob and Mary consented to remain, and their hosts expressed sincere pleasure at the decision.

Pleasant days at the Farm

Jacob and Mary now settled in their own little home and began housekeeping for themselves. A few articles of furniture were got for the living-room, and such cooking utensils as were needed for the kitchen. Mary thought herself very happy in being able to prepare meals for her father, and they led together a life of contentment. While Jacob was making baskets, and Mary was occupied with knitting and sewing, they amused each other with familiar conversation. Sometimes they spent the evening with the farmer and his household, when all were pleased to listen to the old man's amusing and instructive stories and pleasant conversation. Winter, with its storms, passed quickly but in the most agreeable manner.

Near the house was a large garden, which was not very well kept. The farmer and his wife had too much to do on the farm generally to be able to spare any time for the garden; and besides, even if that had not been the case, they did not know enough about the art of gardening to do anything with it.

Jacob, therefore, undertook to cultivate it. He had made the necessary preparations during the autumn, and scarcely had the warmth of spring dissipated the winter's snow than he began the work, assisted by Mary. They worked from early in the morning until quite late in the evening. The garden was laid out in beds; the beds planted with all sorts of vegetables, and flowers such as bees love, and bordered with gravel walks. Mary allowed her father no rest until he had brought her from the village (where he was in the habit of buying the seeds of vegetables) rose-trees, tulip and lily roots, and various kinds of flower seeds. She cultivated the most beautiful flowers, and among them were some which had never been seen in this rough out-of-the-way place. The garden soon exhibited an outburst of greenery and colour. The valley had until then been a gloomy place with dark forest-trees. It now assumed quite a cheerful appearance. The orchard also prospered much better under Jacob's hand, and brought forth richer fruit, as well as in greater abundance. In short, the blessing of Heaven was upon everything Jacob undertook.

The old gardener had now regained his accustomed cheerfulness; and began again to entertain and instruct Mary by his reflections on the flowers. He always found something new to say. During the first spring days Mary had sought for violets along the thicket which bordered their rustic garden. She wished, as usual, to offer the first bunch of them to her father. At last she found some beautiful ones which had a delightful perfume and ran, transported with joy, to present them to him.

"Good!" said her father, taking the flowers with a grateful smile, "seek and ye shall find. But listen," he continued; "it is worthy of notice that this beautiful flower, the lovely violet, delights to grow among brambles. In that we may find a lesson which applies specially to us. Who would have thought that in this dark valley, all covered with woods, and in this old cottage whose thatched roof is green with moss, we should find so much happiness? But there is no situation in life so thorny that some quiet joy may not be discovered hidden among the thorns. Always have a firm trust in God, and in whatever troubles you may suffer, inward peace will never forsake you."

One day a tradesman's wife came from the city to buy some flax of the farmer, and brought her little boy with her. While she was engaged in examining the flax, and in choosing and bargaining, the child, having found the garden gate open, went in, and immediately fell upon a full-blown rose-bush and began to pluck the flowers, with the result that he scratched himself terribly with the thorns. The mother and the farmer's wife ran out into the garden as soon as they heard his cries. Jacob and Mary also hastened to see what was the matter. The child, with his little hands covered with blood, cried passionately, and denounced the rose-tree for having deceived him by its pretty flowers.

"It is sometimes thus with us bigger children," said Jacob. "Pleasures often have their thorns like this rose. We run to grasp them with both hands, and frequently are only made aware of our mistake when too late. We are led away from God and his word then we begin to weep and lament like this boy. We accuse the thing that has caused us harm, while it is ourselves that are to blame. Do not be led to act thoughtlessly because a rose is beautiful. Instead enjoy it in the way that it was intended we should. God has given man reason, a mind, and a conscience in order that he may learn to use things in moderation."

One beautiful morning Mary and her father went into the garden. There had been a couple of days of rain and as they wandered in the garden they found the first lilies in bloom, looking very lovely in the rays of the rising sun. Mary called all the people of the house, who for a long time had been curious to see the lilies in bloom. They were in an ecstasy of admiration.

"How white they are! How pure and spotless!" exclaimed the farmer's wife.

"Indeed they are!" said Jacob with emotion. "If the consciences of men were as pure, what a pleasing sight it would be for God! For a pure heart alone can enter heaven."

"And how beautifully straight and

upright it stands!" remarked the farmer.

"Yes, as straight as a finger that points to heaven," Jacob replied. "I am happy to see this flower in the garden. There ought not to be a garden in the country where the lily is not found. Obliged as we are continually to look to the earth for our food and sustenance, we are sometimes apt to forget heaven. But the fair upright lily should teach us that in the midst of our troubles and labours we should do well to raise our thoughts towards the celestial kingdom, and aspire to something better than the best the earth can give. Every plant," he continued impressively, "even the tenderest blade of grass, has a tendency to grow upwards, and those that are too weak to rise by themselves, such as the bean, and the hop which we see in the hedge, entwine themselves about the first support, and so climb by the aid of another. It would be sad indeed if man, with his hopes, his aspirations, and his knowledge of better things, should alone of all created things be satisfied to creep for ever upon the earth."

Jacob was one day employed in placing young plants in a new-made bed; Mary was weeding at a little distance from him. "Planting and weeding" said the father, "should be the occupation of all our life.

Our heart is a garden which the good God has given us to cultivate. We should be unceasingly employed cultivating the good and uprooting the evil that may enter there. Otherwise it will become a wilderness. But let us scrupulously fulfil these two duties, and seek the assistance and blessing of God who makes the sun to shine, the dew and rain to fall, plants to grow, and the fruit to ripen. Then will our hearts blossom like a well-watered garden, and we shall possess paradise within ourselves."

It was thus that Jacob and Mary led an active and industrious life, mingling instructive conversation with their innocent pleasures. Three springs and three summers had glided away, and the happy days they had spent at Pine Farm had almost caused them to forget their past misfortunes. But when autumn returned again, and the mid-day sun cast longer shadows, while the last ornaments of the garden, the red and blue asters, bloomed, and the many-coloured foliage of the trees showed the approach of winter, Jacob's health began visibly to decline, and he very often felt himself far from well. He, however, concealed his feelings from Mary, fearing it would distress her. His reflections upon the flowers became more and more melancholy, and Mary, who observed this change, felt it to the bottom of her heart.

One morning as she was looking at a rose which had blossomed late, and was considering whether she should gather it, a breath of wind touched it, and it fell to pieces on the ground. "So it is with man," said her father. "In youth we resemble a rose newly opened, but our life fades as the rose. Pride not yourself, my dear child, upon the beauty of the body; it is vain and fragile; but strive after the beauty of the soul - the adornment of goodness which can never fade."

One day, towards evening, Jacob ascended a ladder to gather some apples. He handed them to Mary, who put them carefully in a basket. "How cold," he said, "is the autumn wind that whistles over the stubble field; how it plays with the yellow leaves and with my white hairs! I am in my autumn, my dear Mary, and soon yours will follow. Try to resemble this excellent tree, which produces fruit so valuable, and in such great abundance, so that you may please the master of this great garden, which is called the world."

As Mary was one day sowing some seed for the following spring, her father said: "The day will come when they will put us in the ground as you are putting these seeds, and the soil will cover us. But console yourself, my dear child! After a little while the tiny seed begins to stir in the earth, it shows signs of life, and in the form of a fair flower raises its head above the ground. In the same way we triumph over the grave. We shall one day rise to a new and everlasting life out of the darkness of the tomb. Think of this, my dear Mary, when I am laid to rest; and when you see the flowers which you plant upon my grave springing up to renewed life in the spring, let them be to you an emblem and an assurance of resurrection and immortality."

Mary looked wistfully at her father. Two large tears stood in his eyes, and he seemed greatly changed. She knew that he was thinking of her, and that she would soon be left alone in a world of temptations and sorrows. Sad and painful forebodings filled her heart, and she fell down on her knees by his side and wept with him.

Jacob's Illness

At the beginning of winter, which threatened to be very severe, and which had already covered mountain and valley with snow, Jacob became very ill. Mary begged him to allow the physician of the neighbouring village to come and see him; and immediately the farmer, who was always on the alert to do a kindness, drove over in his sledge to fetch him. The doctor wrote his prescription, and Mary walked with him as far as the door to ask if he had any hope of her father's recovery. He replied that the old man was in no immediate danger but that his disease would turn to consumption, and from that, especially at his age, he could not be expected to recover. At this news Mary nearly fainted. She wept and sobbed, and could hardly be comforted. After a time, however, she became more composed, and wiped away her tears. Before she returned to her father she calmed herself for fear of distressing him.

Mary attended her father with all the care that a good daughter could give to a most beloved parent. She watched his every look in order to anticipate his slightest want, and every night was spent by his bedside. If anyone wished to relieve her for fear that she should herself become sick, and if she, after much persuasion, consented to rest for a few moments on her couch, it very rarely happened that she closed her eyes. Did her father but cough, she trembled; if he made the least stir, she immediately approached him softly and on tiptoe to inquire how he was. With the tenderest love she prepared and brought him the food which best suited his condition. She arranged his pillow, read to him, and prayed for him continually. "Oh, God, leave him with me a little longer, even just for a few years!"

Mary had a little money which she had saved from the work of her own hands. She had earned it by very often spending half the night in sewing and knitting. This she made use of to the last penny in purchasing her father's favourite food - so as to tempt him to eat and thus build up his strength.

The pious old man, although he felt a little stronger, was sure he was on his death-bed. He was calm and perfectly resigned and spoke of his approaching death with the greatest serenity.

Mary cried bitterly, "Do not speak like that. I cannot bear the thought. What would become of me? I would then not have a friend on earth."

"Do not cry, dear child," said her father, holding out his hand to her "you have a kind Father in heaven. He will never forsake you, although your earthly father be taken away from you. I do not feel anxious about how you will live. The birds of the air are supplied with food; why should not you also be provided for? God cares for the smallest sparrow. He will also care for you, who are worth many sparrows! Man's wants are few and for a short time. So as far as your mere material wants are concerned I have no anxiety. It is different when I think of your spiritual welfare. If I could be sure that you would always remain as good and pious and innocent as, thank God, you are now, I should die happy."

Mary sobbed, "Do not fear for me. I

shall always think of you, and be guided by your instruction."

"Alas! my dear child," Jacob replied, "you do not suspect the world of being half so wicked or corrupt as it is, or of containing half so many wicked people as it does. It grieves me to say it, but it is only too true, that there are men in the world who would think it merely a jest to deprive you, my poor girl, of innocence, honour, peace of heart, and the whole happiness of your life. They would call you childish if you spoke of the fear of God, of conscience, the commandments of God, and of eternity. My child, avoid such men! When they flatter you, and call you beautiful, and hover about you as the butterfly round the flower, do not listen to them or take any notice of what they say. Do not accept a present from them. Place no trust in their promises. Under the form of an angel a very Satan is frequently hidden, and beneath the most beautiful flowers a serpent often sleeps. But God has given you for your protection that guardian feeling, modesty. If anyone suggests an evil thought, or even utters a sinful word, in your presence you will feel the glow of modesty mount to your cheek. Take warning from this guardian of innocence. Do not neglect it, lest it leave you for ever. So long as modesty remains, and you listen to its warning, you will not be led astray. Neglect its warning even for once, and you are in danger of being lost forever."

Mary, deeply moved, pressed her father's hand.

"Ah, my dear child," he continued, "you will find even an enemy in your own heart. There will be moments in your life when you will feel a desire for what is evil, and when you may persuade yourself that it is not so very bad, or even that it is unsinful and permissible. But take warning, and let the words of your dying father be deeply engraven upon your heart. My eyes will soon be closed for ever; then I shall be able to watch over you no more. But remember that your heavenly Father, who is everywhere and sees everything, is able also to read the secrets of your heart. You would hate to trouble me, your earthly father, by falling into bad conduct; how much more then should you fear and strive not to offend your Almighty Father who is in heaven?"

After a pause the old man continued: "Look at me once more, Mary; I shall not be much longer with you. Oh, if you should ever be tempted to do wrong, think of my pale face, and of the tears which wet my shrunken cheeks. Promise me never to forget my words. In the hour of temptation imagine you feel this cold hand which you now hold, and which is on the brink of the grave. Poor child, you cannot see without weeping my pale and hollow cheeks. Ah! know that everything passes away in this world. There was a time when I too had the bloom of health, and the fresh complexion you now have. The time will come when you too have to die. It may be many years from now or sooner than you think."

The next day Jacob believing his end was near, felt, though very weak, that it was his duty to continue his dying advice.

"I have seen the world," he said, "as well as other people, when I accompanied the young Count in his travels. Everything in the large cities that was superb or magnificent, I went to see it. I spent whole weeks in pleasure. Brilliant assemblies, or lively conversations, I saw and heard all, as well as my young master. I always had my share in the most dainty meals, and of the choicest wines, and always had more than

I wished for. But all these noisy pleasures left me with an empty heart. A few moments of peaceful contemplation and fervent prayer under our arbour in Terborg, or under that thatch that covers us now, gave me more real joy than all the vain pleasures of this world.

Seek, then, your happiness in the love and service of our blessed Saviour. You will find him, and he will bless you. I have not wanted for misfortunes in this life. Alas! when I lost your mother my heart was for a long time like a dry and barren garden, whose soil, burnt by the heat of the sun, cracks open and seems to sigh for rain. Like this I languished, thirsting for consolation; at last I found it in the Lord.

"There will be days in your life when your heart will be like a dry and barren ground. But do not feel distressed at it. The thirsty ground calls not in vain for rain. God sends the rain. Seek your consolation in the Lord. This consolation will refresh your heart as a sweet rain refreshes the thirsty earth. My dear child, let your confidence in God be unshaken. There is nothing he will not do for those he loves. He gives us grief to lead us to unmingled happiness. Remember all the grief which you felt when, after our painful walk, I fell down with fatigue in the middle of the road? Well, this accident was the means God used to bring us the sweet rest which we have enjoyed for three years with these good people. Without this sickness, we should either not have come before their door, or they would not have been touched with so much compassion. All the pleasures which we have had, all the good which we have been able to do, all the happy days which we have spent here, are a result of this sickness.

"So in the troubles of this life we can find divine goodness. The generous hand of the Lord has scattered flowers on the mountains and valleys, on the forests and the banks of rivers, and even on the muddy marshes, to show us his tenderness and goodness. He has also imprinted on all the events of our life traces of his great wisdom, and of his compassionate love for men, in order that we may learn by them to love and adore Him. Never have we had more to suffer than when you were accused of theft, put in chains - likely to be condemned to death. We were together weeping and lamenting in prison.

"Well, this evil trial has been a source

of good to us. Yes, those blessings are visible now! When the young Countess distinguished you from the other young girls, did you the honour to admit you to her company, made you a present of a beautiful gown, and wished you to be always near her, no doubt you thought yourself very happy. But it was to be feared that those honours, those luxuries, and those vanities would make you vain, fond of the things of this world, and apt to forget God.

But in misery, in poverty, in prison, we have lived near to him; he has taken us away from a corrupt world into this rough country, where he has prepared for you a better dwelling.

You are like a flower which embellishes the most secret places, where it has nothing to fear from the hand of man. It is this good and faithful God, who wishes to give a still more happy turn to the misfortunes which you have suffered.

"Yes, I firmly believe he has answered my prayer - he will one day show the world your innocence. When this time shall come I may be no more; but, convinced as I am of your innocence, I need not to see you justified in order to die in peace.

Yes, Mary, the pain which you have suffered will yet be the means of leading you to joy and happiness on earth. Let not care trouble your soul; believe that God's tenderness watches over you, that his care will be sufficient for you, and in whatever place he chooses to take you to, in whatever painful situation you may be placed, say, 'It is the place - the best situation for me, despite all that I suffer.' Believe that it is exactly the position in which to perfect your virtue, and for you to do the will of your Saviour who died for you."

So much exertion caused the old man to feel faint for a time; but after a few hours he continued his advice.

"A gardener, my dear Mary," he said, "assigns to each plant the spot he thinks will be the most proper to make it prosper. In the same manner God gives to every believer that station in life which suits him best, and in which he will make the greatest progress in holiness. God has until now, Mary, turned to your advantage all your misfortunes, he will also bless to you my last sickness and death. I cannot pronounce the word death without causing you to shed a torrent of tears. But do not think that death is so terrible.

Let us once speak as we used to do in our garden at Terborg. You know what happens at the beginning of spring; small and weak plants sprout out together from narrow and moist beds; it is not then supposed that they will produce beautiful flowers or delicious fruits, and indeed they will bear neither fruits nor flowers if they remain crowded in this narrow space; they will want room; and the gardener who placed them there does not wish them to remain there and die. He designs to transplant them into an open space, where they may be revived by the pure air, and be exposed to the golden rays of the sun. At last, watered by rain and dew, they put forth leaves, and shine in all their beauty. It was always a pleasure to you when I transplanted these young shoots, for you used to say they crowded one another in the beds. You were only satisfied when they were in an open space.

'Now', you would say, 'they will grow finely - I think that I see them do so already.'

"My dear daughter, we are poor weak plants; the earth which we inhabit is a narrow bed; this is not our home - we are destined to become something greater and more perfect. That is the reason why God transplants us into large and beautiful gardens - in a word, to heaven.

"Don't cry. I rejoice to go so soon to my Saviour! What a happiness to be delivered from this body which has done so much evil in the world, and to be with Christ for ever!

Dear Mary, do you remember the great pleasure we took in our garden on a beautiful spring morning?

Heaven is to be compared to the most beautiful of all gardens, where Spring lasts forever. It is for this delightful country I am going to set out.

Continue to serve God, and we shall be there at last united. Here we have been together only to suffer tribulations without number - we have been separated only to weep and lament. But there we shall remain together in the midst of joy and blessing, without the fear of separation.

Mary, always live close to God. If you have a good and happy life here below, let not these passing joys make you forget the joys of eternity. Then your mother and I shall meet our daughter in heaven. Do not weep, my dear child, but rather rejoice in the prospect of the future."

Jacob attempted to console his daughter, who was soon to be left alone on the earth. He tried by his advice, to strengthen her against an evil world. Every word was a good seed which fell on well-prepared ground.

"I have caused you much grief and many tears, my dear child," he said at length; "but seeds sown among tears take root more easily, and thrive better than when no deep emotion is stirred; they are like grain which when sown is watered by the soft showers of spring."

The death of Jacob

When Mary found that her father could not survive much longer, she went to Erlenbrunn, the parish to which Pine Farm belonged, and informed the pastor of the illness of her father. Being an exemplary and pious man he paid Jacob a number of visits, and had some good conversations with him. He also never failed to say a few words of comfort and encouragement to Mary. One afternoon when he paid his visit, he found the old man very much weaker. Jacob requested Mary to leave the room for a moment, in order that he might have a few minutes' conversation with the pastor alone. He soon called her in again and said, "My dear Mary, I have now settled all my worldly affairs, I am ready to die."

Mary was much distressed, and had

great difficulty in restraining her tears, for she saw that the fatal moment was not far off.

Jacob spent the remainder of the day and evening in silent prayer. He spoke little. Next day, he took holy communion at the hands of the pastor with indescribable joy. Faith, love, and the hope of eternal life cheered him, tears of joy ran down his cheeks. Mary, on her knees beside his bed, trembled, wept and prayed. The farmer, his wife, and all their household contemplated this solemn scene with deep emotions. Almost every eye was wet with tears.

"Now," said Mary afterwards, "I feel as though my heart has been relieved of a burden. I am greatly consoled. It is indeed true that Jesus Christ consoles and strengthens us not only in life, but even at the hour of death."

Meanwhile Jacob felt his end rapidly approaching. The farmer and his wife, who honoured and cherished him as their best friend, and blessed the day that brought him into their house, did everything they could think of to comfort him in his last hours. Ten times a day would they come - now one and now the other - to inquire how he was; and each time Mary would inquire with mingled grief and affection in her voice: "Don't you think that he may yet recover?"

Once the farmer's wife gave her for answer, "Oh! my child, I do not think that he can hold out longer than the coming of the leaves on the trees."

From that time Mary continually sat at her little window, and trembling, watched the budding of the flowers in her garden. The return of spring had always filled her with joy; but now the leaves of the gooseberry bushes and the budding of the trees filled her with sadness. The joyous chirping of the chaffinch overwhelmed her with terror; and when she saw the flowers of the snowdrop and the primrose she was deeply affected.

"Everything is renewed - everything in nature smiles! Must my dear father be without hope and die?" she asked. And then checking herself, she raised her eyes to heaven, and said, "no, not without hope! no, no! Jesus has said he shall not die - 'he that believeth in me shall not die'. He only puts off this earthly body, this house of clay, in order that he may enjoy a new and better life in heaven above."

It gave the old man great pleasure to

hear Mary read to him, she did it in so sweet and clear a voice. During the latter part of his illness he liked to hear nothing better than the last words of Jesus, and his last prayer. Once during the night his daughter was sitting beside his bed; the beams of the moon shone so brightly into the room that the light of the candle was scarcely visible.

"Mary," said the invalid, "read again that beautiful prayer of our Saviour."

Opening her father's Bible she read as he desired.

"Now," said he, "give me the book, and hold the light a little nearer to me." Mary gave him the book, and placed the candle so that it lighted the page.

"Now," said he, "this will be the last prayer that I shall make for you." He marked the passage with his finger, and prayed in a trembling voice: "O Father, I have not long to remain in this world, but this, my child, will be left here for a little while. I am coming - I dare to hope - to thee, Father! But before I go, holy and almighty God, I ask thee once more to preserve my child from sin, for thy name's sake. While I have been on earth, I have tried in thy name to preserve her from this wicked world. But,

O Lord, I am now coming to thee. I do not ask thee to take her to thee, but only to preserve her from harm. Let thy holy truth support her. Thy word is truth. Grant, O heavenly Father, that the child which thou hast given me may at last come to where I hope to go, through Jesus my Saviour. Amen."

Mary, who stood beside his bed bathed in tears, repeated as well as her sobs would allow her, "Amen."

"Yes," he continued, "my dear daughter. We shall see Jesus in his kingdom, which he had from the beginning of the world. There we shall once more meet each other."

He laid himself down on his pillow to rest a little. He continued to hold the Bible in his hand. It was one he had bought since he left Terborg, with the first money saved from his scanty earnings.

"Dear Mary," he said some moments afterwards, "I thank you again most sincerely for all the affection and tenderness which you have shown me since my illness commenced. You have faithfully observed the fifth commandment. Bear in mind the promise given to those who honour and obey their parents. I believe, my dear child, that it will be fulfilled to you, though I am obliged to leave you poor and helpless. I can give you nothing but my blessing and this book. Be always pious and good, and this blessing will not be without effect. My blessing and the Lord is better than the richest inheritance. Take this Bible, and let it be a remembrance of your father. It cost me, it is true, but a few shillings, but let it be faithfully read and put into practice, and then I shall have left you the richest treasure. If I had left you as many pieces of gold as the spring produces leaves and flowers, with all that money you could not buy anything better; for this book contains the word of God. Read it every morning - no matter what work you have to do, time should always be found for that - read at least one passage - preserve it and meditate upon it in your heart during the day. If you discover any obscurity, pray for the Holy Spirit to enlighten you, as I have always done, and with infinite profit. All that is most essential in the book may be understood by everybody. Hold fast to that, follow it faithfully, and it will not fail to give you the blessing of Heaven. This passage alone, 'Consider the lilies of the field', has given me more wisdom than all the books which I read in my youth; and besides that, it has been the source to me of a thousand pleasures. My many sorrows would have filled me with unceasing anxiety. I should have been endlessly discouraged and dejected. But this passage gave me the foundation for a serene and happy spirit."

About three o'clock in the morning Jacob faintly said, "I feel very ill - open the window a little."

Mary opened it; the moon had disappeared, but the sky, covered with stars, presented a magnificent spectacle. "See how beautiful the sky appears!" said the sick man. "What are the flowers of the earth compared with those stars. It is there I am now going. Oh, what joy! I am going to my Lord and Saviour! Keep close to Him, my dear child and we shall meet again!"

As he uttered these words he fell upon his bed and died the death of a Christian.

Mary thought he had only fainted, for she had never seen anyone die, and did not think he was so near his end; nevertheless in her fright she awoke all the family; they ran to the old man's bed-side, and then she heard them declare he was dead. Mary ran to the bedside and wept bitterly.

"Oh, my father - my good father," she

cried, "how shall I repay you for all the goodness you have shown to me? I can only thank you for all the words, for all the good advice that I have from your mouth, your lips, now sealed in death. It is with gratitude that I kiss your hand, now cold and stiff - that hand which bestowed on me so many benefits, which laboured so much for my good, and which in my childhood chastised me with so much loving-kindness. I now see for the first time how well meant it was, and how good it was for me. Oh, receive my thanks - receive my heartfelt thanks for all your goodness, and forgive me for my childish thoughtlessness! Oh, God, repay him for all his love to me! When my time comes, 'let me die the death of the righteous', as this man, my father, has done! How little - how very little there is in this life on earth! How good it is that there is a heaven, and an everlasting life! That is now my only consolation."

The scene was heartrending. At last the farmer's wife, after entreating Mary for some time, prevailed upon her to lie down. Nothing would induce her during the following day to leave the body of her father. She read, wept, and prayed alternately the night though. Before the coffin lid was nailed down, Mary took one more look at her father. "It is the last time that I shall ever see that beloved face. How beautiful it was when you smiled. Farewell, my father!" she cried.

She gathered rosemary, primroses as yellow as gold, and violets of a deep blue. Making a bouquet of them she placed them by her father, who during his life had sown and cultivated so many flowers.

When they began to nail down the coffin lid, every stroke of the hammer caused her grief.

Mary attended the funeral of her father in a deep mourning dress lent to her for the occasion by a sympathetic woman in the village. She followed close to the body of her father. Her face was as pale as death, and every one pitied the poor forsaken orphan, who now had neither father or mother.

As Mary's father was a stranger in the district, they dug a grave for him in the corner of the cemetery against the wall. Beside this wall were two large pine-trees which shaded the tomb. The pastor preached a touching sermon from the text: "Except a corn of wheat fall into the ground and die, it abideth alone; but if it die, it bringeth forth much fruit," John 12:24. He spoke of Jacob's patience, the resignation with which he had borne all his misfortunes, and the good example he had set to those who knew him. He said a few words of consolation to Mary. He thanked, in the name of the deceased, the farmer and his wife, who had looked after Mary and her father so well. In short, he begged them to be father and mother to Mary, who had no longer any parents.

Later whenever Mary attended a church service she never failed to visit the tomb. She would go every Sunday evening, when the opportunity offered, to visit the grave of her father, and to weep. "Nowhere," would she say, "have I prayed with so much fervour as here at my father's grave. Here the whole world is nothing to me. I feel that we belong to a better world. My heart sighs for that country, because I daily feel the evil of the world in which I now am." She never left the grave without having made good resolutions to despise the pleasures of the world, and to live for her God.

Mary still sowing in tears

From the time of her father's death Mary was constantly sad. The flowers had in her eyes lost all their beauty; and the pines near the farm looked as though they were clothed in black. Time, it is true, moderated her grief, but soon she had new trials to undergo.

Great changes had taken place at Pine Farm since the death of her father. The farmer had given up the farm to his only son, a man of good temper and amiable disposition, but unhappy in the choice of his wife, whom he had married a short time before. People thought her beautiful and she was possessed of considerable property. But she was vain of her beauty, and cared for nothing but money. Pride and greed could be seen even in her facial expressions. She appeared to have a harshness that was very striking. So with all her comeliness her looks were repulsive. She did not believe in the Lord Jesus Christ. She did not follow the good ways of the gospel. If she knew that anything would give the old people pleasure, she did just the contrary. Even when she gave them their food, which was their due according to the contract they had made between them, it was always done grudgingly and with a bad grace. The old farmer and his wife had been promised that they would be looked after for the remainder of their days. But their son's wife sought continually to belittle them. She made their lives miserable to the last degree. The poor old couple retired into the little back chamber, and seldom appeared in the front room.

The young husband, too, was no happier than his parents; the wicked woman overwhelmed him with the grossest abuse, and cast into his teeth a hundred times a day the money she had brought him. If he would not spend the day in quarrelling and disputing, he was obliged to suffer in silence. She would never quietly allow him to visit his parents, for fear, as she said, he would give them something secretly. In the evening, after he had finished his work, he scarcely dared to go near them. He found them almost always seated side by side in the utmost sadness. He would take a seat by them, and complain of his hard lot.

"Well, well," replied the old man, "such is the way of the world. Your mother allowed herself to be dazzled by the glitter of her gold; you were taken by her rosy cheeks; I yielded too easily to your wishes, and thus we are all punished. We should have thought of the good advice of old Jacob; he was an experienced man, and never approved of this match when it was talked of during his life. I still remember every word he said on the subject, and I have thought of it more than a thousand times. Do you remember," he said, turning to his wife, "having one day said, 'But ten thousand florins is worth having! It is a beautiful sum of money!'"

The old woman said she remembered.

"And well do I recollect Jacob's answer," continued the old farmer. "'Do not call it a beautiful sum,' he said. 'The flowers you see in your garden are a thousand times more beautiful. Perhaps you meant to say it is a large and heavy sum. I will acknowledge that. He must have good shoulders who can bear it without being bowed down to the earth, without becoming a poor wretch, unable to raise his head to heaven. Why then wish for so much money? You have never wanted for anything; so far from it, you have always had more than enough. Believe me, to have too much money is no blessing; it is as bad as having too little. Rain is useful and necessary; but when too much falls there is great danger of its destroying the most healthy plants of the garden.'

"These are exactly the words of the old friend we have lost; I fancy I can still hear him. And you, my son, once said to him, 'She is a charming girl, as beautiful and fresh as a rose.' 'Flowers,' answered the wise old man, 'have not beauty only - they are useful and pretty at the same time. They make us many rich presents; and the bee extracts from them pure wax and delicious honey. Without piety, a beautiful exterior is but a rose upon paper, a miserable trifle, without life and without perfume, which produces neither wax or honey.' Such were the reflections which Jacob made before us. We would not listen to him - now we appreciate his advice. That which appeared to us then so great a happiness is now to us the height of misfortune. God give us the grace to bear our misfortunes with patience."

Thus they used frequently to talk together.

As to poor Mary she also had much to suffer. The old people were obliged to occupy the back room. She therefore gave up her place to them. The young wife had two rooms empty, but through unkindness she gave Mary the most miserable apartment in the house, ill-treated her in every possible way, and loaded her with abuse. There was nothing but fault-finding from morning till night. Mary, according to her, did not work enough, and did not know how to do anything as it ought to be done. It was very plainly to be seen by the poor orphan that she was despised, and a trouble to the house. The old man and his wife were not in a situation to offer her any consolation; they had enough to do with their own griefs. She thought often of going away, but where to go she knew not. She asked the pastor's advice.

"My dear Mary," said the good man, "to remain any longer at the Pine Farm is a thing impossible. Your father gave you an excellent education, and had you trained in everything that is necessary for the management of a tradesman's family. But at Pine Farm they put more hard work upon you than a rough country girl, used to the toil of a farm, could do. The labour they require of you is beyond your strength, and is not suited to your training or condition. However, I would not advise you to leave immediately. You would be quite alone in the wide world and who knows if you would find a situation that would be more agreeable to you. The best advice I can give you is, to remain where you are for the present; to work as much as you can, and to wait patiently until the Lord shall deliver you. The Saviour who raised you to another condition is still able to sustain you. I will try to get you a place in an honest, Christian family. Pray unceasingly; have confidence in God; bear your trials with patience, and God will arrange all things for your good."

Mary thanked him, and promised to follow his good advice.

In all her troubles there was one spot where Mary could always find comfort and solace; it was the grave of her father. There she seemed to be brought nearer to him.

There she would remember all his kindly advice and wise instruction. She had planted a rose-tree there. "Alas!" she mourned, as she planted the shrub, "if I could remain here always, I would water you with my tears, and you would soon be covered with flowers and leaves."

The rose-tree was already covered with leaves, and the tender buds began to open their crimson cups. "My father was right," said Mary, "when he compared human life to a rose-tree. Sometimes it is quite withered and bare; it offers to the eye nothing but thorns. But wait a little, and the season will return when it will be clothed anew with foliage, and adorned with the most beautiful flowers. This is now for me the time of thorns, but God forbid that I should be cast down by it. I believe your word, O God. You are the best of fathers."

The Last and Heaviest Trial

In the midst of all Mary's troubles, the 25th of July arrived, the anniversary of her father's birthday. Until then it had always been to her a day of joy, but this time when she woke, she woke with tears in her eyes. In former days she had always prepared for this day something which she knew would give her father pleasure; but now he was gone. The country people in the neighbourhood were in the habit of ornamenting with flowers the graves of their dearest friends, particularly at the time of such anniversaries. They had often entreated Mary to give them flowers, and she always took pleasure in gratifying their wishes. She now thought of decorating her father's tomb in the same manner. The beautiful though ill-fated basket, which had been the first cause of her unhappiness, was standing before her on the cupboard.

Mary took it and filled it with flowers of all colours and with fresh leaves, carried it to Erlenbrunn an hour before the service, and deposited it on her father's grave. Her tears fell upon the flowers, and glittered like dew upon the fresh leaves. "Father," she said, "you filled my life with flowers. If I cannot do as much for you, I will at least decorate your grave with them." Mary left the basket on the tomb; she had no fear that any one would dare to steal either the basket or the flowers. At a little distance the country people contemplated this offering with joy mingled with pity, blessed in their hearts Jacob's pious daughter, and prayed for her prosperity.

The following day, as the people of the farm were making hay in a large meadow situated beyond the forest, a piece of fine linen, which was spread out to bleach on the grass near a rivulet a few steps from the house, suddenly disappeared. The young farmer's wife did not miss it until the evening. Being very suspicious, as all misers are, she immediately blamed Mary. Honest Jacob had made no secret of the unfortunate story of the ring, but had confided every circumstance connected with it to the old farmer and his wife. Their son, who had heard it, imprudently related it to his wife. In the evening, when Mary, entered the house with the servants, the wicked woman came out of the kitchen, and met her with a torrent of abuse, and ordered her to produce the linen immediately.

Mary answered gently that it was impossible she could have taken the linen. She had spent the whole day in the hayfield with the other work-people and besides a stranger might easily have taken advantage of a moment when no one was in the kitchen to commit the theft. This conjecture was indeed the truth. The farmer's wife, however, would not listen to reason, but cried out in a paroxysm of rage. "You thief! Do you think I don't know of the theft of the ring and what difficulty you had to escape the hands of the executioner? Get out of the house this instant. There is no room under my roof for such as you!"

"It is too late," said the husband, "to send her away tonight. The sun has already set. Let her sup with us, as she has worked all day in the greatest heat, and must be hungry and tired. In the morning she can go away if you still wish it."

"Not even an hour," said the wicked woman, "shall she stay in my house. And you had better hold your tongue or I will stop your mouth with a burning stick from the fire."

The poor man saw that anything he could say would irritate her still more, and was therefore silent. Mary made no answer to the accusations of the farmer's wife. She wrapped up the little she possessed in a clean napkin, quite large enough to contain all, put the little bundle under her arm, thanked the inhabitants of the Pine Farm for the services they had done her, protested once more her innocence, and asked permission to take leave of the old people who had been her benefactors. "You may do that," said the woman, with a disdainful smile; "and if you would take them with you it would give me great pleasure. It is evident that death is in no hurry to rid me of them."

The good old people had heard the disturbance, and both wept for Mary's sake. They consoled her and gave her what money they had to assist her on her way. "Go, good girl," they said to her, "and may God be with you. The blessing of your father is a precious treasure for you, and one of these days will bring you happiness. Remember us kindly in your prosperity, for things will yet go well with you."

Mary set out with her little bundle under her arm, and began to climb up the mountain, following a narrow road in the woods. She wished to visit once more her father's grave.

When she came out of the forest the village clock struck seven, and before she arrived at the graveyard it was nearly dark; but she was not afraid to pass the night in the midst of the graves. She went to her father's tomb, and her tears fell in torrents.

The full moon shone through the dark foliage of the two pines, and illumined, with a silver light, the roses on the grave, and the basket of flowers.

A gentle breeze blew with a soft murmur among the branches of the pine-trees. The leaves of the rose-tree planted on the tomb, trembled.

"My dear father," said Mary, "why are you not here to hear my complaints?

But I thank God, that you cannot see me like this. You are now happy, and free from sorrow.

But why am I not with you? When we

were driven from the country that we loved you at least were still with me. I had in you a good father, a protector, and faithful friend. Now I have no one. I am alone in the world with nowhere to lay my head. Soon I will not even be able to come here to your grave."

At these words she began again to weep.

"Oh, gracious God!" she cried, as she sank upon her knees, "kind Father in heaven have pity upon me. Show me that thy arm is not shortened - that you are still as mighty as ever.

Don't leave me Lord. I have no one to help me but thou. Take me home to heaven, where my good parents are, or send some comfort to me! When the flowers are weak and drooping after the heat of the day, you send refreshing dew to revive them. Have pity on me!"

When she had become a little calmer she asked herself "What shall I do? It's too late to ask for shelter. If I say how I have been turned out of the house nobody would receive me."

She looked round her. Against the churchyard wall was a gravestone, very old and covered with moss. As the inscription on it had long since faded away, it had been put on one side, and used as a seat.

"I will sit down on this stone," she said, "and pass the night near the tomb of my father. It may be the last time I shall ever be here. In the morning, before the break of day, I will go out once more into the wide world, trusting God to lead me where he would have me go."

Help comes from Heaven

Mary sat on the stone by the wall under the pine tree, which covered her with its dark branches. She hid her face in her handkerchief, all bathed in tears. Her soul was troubled. She prayed, long and hard.

"Oh, heavenly Father," she sobbed, "have you no angel to show me the way that I should go?"

Scarcely had she finished when she heard a sweet voice calling her familiarly by her name, "Mary, Mary." She looked up and trembled with fear. Before her, in the beautiful moonlight, stood a fair and lovely form, with eyes beaming and clothed in a long flowing white robe. Mary sank, frightened and trembling, on her knees, and cried, "Has God really sent an angel from heaven to help me!"

125

"Dear Mary," said a gentle, kind voice, "be not alarmed. I am not an angel from heaven, I am only a mortal like yourself; but I come all the same to help you. God has heard your prayers. Look at me; is it possible you do not know me?"

With an exclamation of surprise Mary cried, "Is it you - the Countess Amelia? Oh, how did you get here, to so frightful a place, at this hour of night, so far from you home?"

The young Countess raised Mary gently from the ground, pressed her to her heart, and kissed her tenderly.

"Dear Mary," she said, "we have done you a great injustice. You have been ill rewarded for the pleasure you once gave me by the present of the basket of flowers. But at last your innocence has been established. Oh, can you forgive us? Can you forgive my parents and me? Come, we are ready to make it up to you, if we can, for all the wrongs that you have suffered. Forgive us, dear Mary."

"Do not speak so my lady," said Mary. "You were very patient towards me, considering the circumstances. I have never felt resentment towards you. I only thought with gratitude of your kindness.

My only sorrow was that you and your dear parents should regard me as an ungrateful and wicked girl. What I longed for was that you might one day be convinced of my innocence, and this prayer God has now granted. Thanks be to Him!"

The Countess pressed Mary to her heart, and bathed her face in tears. Then she looked down at the grave at her feet. Tears pricked her eyes as she saw the name on the headstone, "I wish I could see his face to ask pardon for all the injury we so unjustly did. If we had only taken more precautions and placed more confidence in an old and loyal servant, he would not now be lying here. Oh Jacob if only I could hear you forgive us! But as that cannot be, I solemnly vow that the atonement we can no longer make to you shall be made in double measure to your daughter. Would that we could have been sure of his forgiveness!" exclaimed Amelia in conclusion.

"Ah! gracious lady," said Mary, "my father was very far from feeling the least resentment towards the family he served so long. He included you in his prayers every evening and morning, as he was accustomed to do while we lived in

Terborg. He blessed you all at the hour of his death. 'Mary,' he said, a little while before he died, 'I feel perfectly confident that those whom we served will one day recognise your innocence, and will recall you from exile. Assure, then, the noble Count, the kind-hearted Countess, and the dear Amelia, whom I so often carried in my arms when she was a child, that my heart was full of deepest respect, of love, and gratitude towards them till my last breath.' Be assured, my dear lady, those were his last words."

"Come, Mary," said she, "come and sit down here beside me on this stone. I cannot leave your father's grave till I have told you now God has brought to light your innocence.

The hand of Providence

"God is surely with you, dear Mary," said the young Countess, after they had seated themselves upon the tomb. "He has taken you under his protection. It is he who led me here to assist you. There is nothing but what is simple and natural in this story which I shall give you. You will, however, see in it a chain of truly providential circumstances.

"From the time your innocence was made known to us," she continued, "I had no more happiness. You and your father were always present to my mind. Believe me, dear Mary, I have shed many tears on your account. My parents sought for you everywhere, but without being able to obtain any trace of you. Three days ago I came with my father and mother to the hunting lodge belonging to the Prince which is situated in the forest, not far from the village. It has not been inhabited for twenty years, except by a forester who acts as caretaker. My father, as you know, is the keeper of the royal forests, and he had a dispute relating to a question of boundary to settle. This it what brought him here. He spent the whole of today in the forest, in company with two strange gentlemen who are concerned in the affair. These noblemen came accompanied by their wives and a young lady, the daughter of one of them, and Mother was obliged to devote the evening to their entertainment. It had been extremely warm during the day, and the evening was cool and pleasant. The setting sun was spectacular, the mountains covered with pine forests looked so inviting that I begged Mother's permission to take a short walk. The gamekeeper's daughter came with me.

"As we passed through the village we found the gate of the churchyard open. The tombstones were gilded by the rays of the setting sun. I have always been interested in reading inscriptions and epitaphs: I am moved when one tells of a young man or woman carried off in the bloom of their youth; I experience a melancholy pleasure if I find it records the death of a man or woman who had reached an exceptionally advanced age. Even the verses that I read on the headstones I store up in my memory.

"We went, therefore, into the churchyard. After I had read a great number of the inscriptions, the gamekeeper's daughter said to me, 'I want to show you something very beautiful; it is the grave of an old man. You will find there neither tombstone nor epitaph, but it has been most tastefully adorned with flowers by his daughter who loved him most tenderly. Do you see, through the thick foliage of these pines, a beautiful rose-tree, and a pretty basket of flowers placed on the grave?

"I went to the spot, and stood petrified with amazement. At the first glance I recognized the basket which had been in my mind's eye a thousand times since you left Terborg. I drew near to look at it, and if I had had any doubts, the initials of my name and the arms of my family would have removed them. I questioned my companion about your history, and that of your father. She told me you had been residing at Pine Farm, and related to me some particulars of the last sickness and death of your father, and the grief which it had caused you. I hastened to see the pastor, whom I found a very worthy man. He confirmed all that I had heard, and praised you very, very much. I wished then to go to Pine Farm, but while I was talking with the clergyman time had flown so rapidly that it was already quite dark.

"'What is to be done?' said I; 'it is now too late to go to the farm, and tomorrow at day-break we leave the neighbourhood.'

"Then the pastor sent for the schoolmaster, and asked him to go and bring you without delay to the parsonage.

"'Do you mean the poor stranger, Mary?' asked the schoolmaster when the clergyman had told him what he wished him to do. 'There is no need to go as far as the farm to fetch her. She went a little while ago to her father's grave, and there she is weeping and lamenting, poor child.' He said, 'I fear she will go out of her mind through grief. I saw her from an opening in the steeple when I went to wind up the clock.'

"The pastor wished to accompany me to your father's grave; but I begged him to allow me to go alone, so that I might speak to you freely without witnesses. Yielding to my wishes he went to tell my parents where I was, lest they should be anxious, and to prepare them for your arrival. This will account, my dear Mary, for my sudden and somewhat strange appearance. God with this basket of flowers has reunited us at your father's grave."

"Yes," said Mary, clasping her hands, and raising her grateful eyes to heaven. "God has done it all. He has had pity on my tears. Oh, what goodness - what loving-kindness he has shown towards me!"

"I have still one more circumstance to tell you, my dear Mary," answered the Countess, interrupting her; "one feature of this history appears to me singularly touching and inspires me with the greatest awe for the justice of God, who often directs our lot unknown to ourselves. Juliette, the greatest enemy you have upon earth, had but one thought, one desire, which was to banish you from my heart, and to confirm herself in your place. It was with this view that she invented the wicked falsehood she told, and her atrocious plot appeared to her to have succeeded to perfection. But it was this falsehood that in the end caused her to lose her place, and our confidence, and that rendered you more dear than ever to our hearts. She tried to estrange you for ever from me. Your banishment was a continued subject of triumph to her. In the excess of her malignant joy she went and threw at your feet this basket with an insulting laugh; and it was this event which was destined afterwards to reunite us for ever. If it was not for this basket I would not have discovered you here. It is true that if we love God we have nothing to fear from those who would do evil, for God knows how to turn to our advantage all the ill that wicked people can do to us. Even our most cruel enemies can do nothing to harm us.

"But now that I have told you all this," continued the young Countess, after a pause, "you must tell me, my dear Mary, the reason for your coming so late to your father's grave, and why you were crying so bitterly."

Mary related the circumstances that led to her being driven from the farm, which caused the Countess fresh astonishment and grief.

"But never mind!" said Amelia, "your being sent away led to our meeting all the quicker." Then, after a pause, she added, "It was by God's will that I arrived here just at the time when you were plunged into deepest distress. God knows how to turn evil to good. The farmer's wicked wife, who drove you from her house, thought she would make you unhappy; but she has sent you back to me and my parents, who all desire to make you happy. But it is time for us to be going," Amelia continued: "my parents will be waiting for me. Come, dear Mary, I will never leave you again, and tomorrow you must return with us to Terborg."

Mary could not help feeling a pang of grief at the thought that she might never again have the opportunity to look upon her father's grave, and it was with difficulty that she dragged herself away from the silent churchyard.

Amelia at length took her gently by the arm, and said kindly, "Come! come away, my dear Mary, and bring with you the basket of flowers, so that you may always have a memento of your dear father. We will have a more lasting monument erected. That, I am sure, will please you. Come, you must be impatient to hear the history of the ring, which I will relate to you as we go along."

Amelia put her arm through Mary's, and in the bright moonlight the two walked together towards the old lodge.

How Mary's Innocence was discovered

A long avenue of tall old linden-trees led to the lodge. After Amelia and Mary had walked along for some time in silence the young Countess said, "I must now tell you how the ring was found.

"We left the capital this year earlier than usual, as business required my father's presence at Terborg. We arrived there amid beautiful spring weather in the early days of March. We had not been there many days, however, before the weather changed. One night in particular we had a tremendous storm. You will remember the enormous pear-tree we had in our garden in Terborg. It was already very old, and bore scarcely any fruit. The wind, which that night blew with great violence, damaged and caused it to lean over so much that it threatened every moment to fall. My father therefore ordered it to be cut down. All the servants were obliged to assist, in order that it might be felled with such care as not to injure the other trees in its fall. My mother and father, we children, and indeed all the people in the castle had come into the garden to see the last of the old tree.

"When the tree had come down with a great crash my two little brothers ran to seize a nest of magpies which was in the tree, and which had been for a long time an object of great curiosity to them. They now examined it with great attention. 'Look, brother,' said Augustus, 'what is that shining so brightly amongst the mass of twigs?' 'It sparkles like,' said Albert, 'gold and precious stones.'

"Juliette, always inquisitive, ran forward to look. Then with a shrill cry, she exclaimed, 'It is the ring!' and became as pale as death.

"The boys released the ring from twigs with which it had been interwoven, and carried it immediately, in great glee, to my mother.

"'Yes, it is the ring,' said my mother. 'Oh, good, honest Jacob! Oh poor Mary what injustice we have done you! I am very glad to find the ring again; but I should be much more so if I could find Jacob and Mary. Willingly would I give the ring to be able to make good the wrong we have done them.'

"'But,' said I, 'by what singular chance came the ring to be carried into the nest at the top of the tree?'

"'I can soon explain that to you,' said the old huntsman, Anthony, with tears in his eyes, so great was his joy at seeing your innocence acknowledged. 'Neither the old gardener Jacob, nor his daughter Mary, could have hidden the ring in this place; that is very clear. The tree was too high for either of them to have climbed to its summit, where the nest was. Besides, there was not time for them to have done it. Mary had scarcely returned to the house, after leaving the castle, when she and her father were both arrested. But magpies are well known for their liking for anything that is bright and sparkling; and if they come across light articles of the kind they immediately steal them. They carry them off to their nest. Doubtless one of the birds stole the ring and carried it to the tree. That is very plain. The only thing that astonishes me is, that an old huntsman like myself should not have thought before that the birds might have stolen the ring. But it must have been the will of God to send this great trial to my old friend Jacob and to his daughter Mary.'

"'Anthony,' said my mother, 'you are perfectly right, and the whole thing is now quite clear to me. I recollect distinctly that these birds very often flew down from the top of the old pear-tree on to the window-sill - that the sash was up when the ring disappeared - that the table upon which I had put the ring was close to the window - and that, after having shut the door and bolted it, I went into the next room, where I stayed for some time. Beyond doubt one of the mischievous birds spied the ring from the top of the tree, and took advantage of the few minutes I was in the adjoining room to seize and carry it off unperceived to his nest.'

"My father was much troubled and distressed on seeing such complete and unexpected proof brought to light of your and your father's unjust condemnation.

"'It pains me to the heart,' he said, 'that so great an injury should have been done to these good people. My only consolation is, that it was not done through ill-will but in ignorance and error. I shall never be able to rest until these poor people have been found, their innocence proclaimed to the world, and some atonement made for the injustice they have suffered.'

"Thereupon he turned to Juliette, who stood, pale and trembling, more like a condemned criminal than anything else, while all around were rejoicing that an injustice had been brought to light.

"'You false and deceitful creature!' he cried, 'what can have induced you to lie to your master and to the judge, and thus lead us to do an action the iniquity of which cries to heaven? How could you be so wicked as to bring such cruel and undeserved suffering upon an old man and his poor, innocent daughter?

"'Arrest her this instant!' he said, turning to a couple of constables, who had assisted in cutting down the tree, and who had already approached Juliette, having watched my father in anticipation of the command he now gave. 'Let her be loaded with chains,' said he, in a grave tone - 'the same chains that Mary bore, and let her be thrown into the same prison in which she caused Mary to languish. She shall suffer all that Mary so undeservedly suffered. All that she possesses, whether in money or clothes, shall be taken from her, to serve as a compensation, if that is still possible, to the unhappy people whom she has caused to suffer so unjustly. Lastly, the same officer who conducted Mary and her father out of my dominions shall also conduct Juliette, just as she is, over the borders.'

"These words made everyone present tremble. They were all pale and silent. No one had ever seen my father so angry. A profound silence reigned for some time. But when at length he went into the castle everyone began to speak at once.

"'It is well done,' said the officer, taking Juliette by the arm. 'He who digs a grave for another invariably falls into it himself.'

'That is what you get for telling lies,' said the other officer, taking her other arm. 'No thread is so fine that it cannot be seen in the sunshine.'

"'It was a pretty dress given to Mary,' said the cook in her turn, 'that made Juliette angry. In her passion, not knowing well what she was about, she began to tell lies. Once she told one lie she had to tell another lie to cover for the last one - until she was too deep to dig herself out. It's just like what the old proverb says, "When Satan has got us by the hair, he will lead us to destruction"'

"'Juliette has got what she deserves,' said the coachman, who had been one of those to put an axe to the root of the tree, and who still held the instrument over his shoulder. 'Let us hope that at least this time she will mend her ways, if she does not wish to be worse off in the next world. The tree that bears not good fruit,' said he, shaking his axe, 'shall be cut down, and cast into the fire.'

"The news of the finding of the ring quickly spread through all Terborg, and everyone ran to the palace to ask if it was true. In a little while quite a crowd had collected. Amongst others came the magistrate who tried and condemned Mary and her father. His clerk had heard of the discovery, and had hastened to tell him of it.

"You can scarcely imagine, my dear Mary, the effect that this story produced on the good man; despite his severity towards you he is a man of honour and has been distinguished all his life for his truthfulness and good conduct.

"'I would give half my fortune,' he said, in a tone that went to the heart of all present, 'nay, I would willingly have given everything that I possess, for this not to have happened. It is a terrible thing to condemn an innocent person unjustly.' Then, looking round him at the assembled people, he said, in a loud and solemn voice,

'God is the only judge who never errs, and whom no one can deceive. He alone knew how the ring disappeared. He alone knew the place in which it has remained hidden until now. The judges of the earth are very liable to err through short-sightedness. Here on earth, unfortunately, innocence must often suffer and guilt come off victorious.

But God, the invisible Judge, who will one day judge all hearts, and reward the good and punish the wicked, has in this case been pleased to clear the innocent and bring to justice the guilty. This dreadful storm, which shook the whole castle made us all tremble last night, but it bent the old tree until it was ready to fall. A heavy and sudden shower washed the inside of the nest clean so that the ring might sparkle and attract attention. Then the Count and his family were at the castle came out into the garden to witness the cutting down of the tree. See, again that it was the two innocent and frolicsome boys, the young counts who discovered the ring.

They would not have thought of hiding it. And then Juliette herself, the false accuser, was the first to make known Mary's innocence by the piercing cry she uttered upon seeing the ring.

"'This,' the venerable magistrate continued, 'though surprising, is by no means an extraordinary development of events. God was in control and he worked it all out. In the world to come God will once more take up and retry all the cases in which men have have been judged in this world, and will give justice to each according to the right, whether the verdict be eternal death or life everlasting in the heavens. Do not lose faith in an eternal, all-directing all-powerful God, who rules everything in truth and righteousness.'

"The magistrate spoke so solemnly. Every one listened to him with great attention, and when he had ceased, everyone went back quietly to their homes, deeply moved by what he had said. So now, dear Mary, I have told you the whole story of the finding of the ring and the establishment of your innocence."

By this time the young Countess and Mary had reached the gate of the lodge.

Virtue Rewarded

The Count and the Countess, and the other guests staying at the old hunting-lodge were assembled in the drawing-room, which was decorated with taste and even magnificence, in accordance with the fashion of the olden times. The walls were hung with tapestry, upon which were depicted scenes from the chase, with the huntsmen, horses, dogs, stags, and wild boars, all so life-like and true to nature, that at the first glance, and especially at night when the room was brilliantly lighted with scores of candles, one seemed to be in the glades of the forest itself, so fresh were the colours and so artistic the work.

The worthy pastor had been some time at the lodge, and all the company had listened with great interest to what he had been saying of Jacob and Mary. He had told the story of the pious old man with so much feeling that all were greatly moved. He also gave numerous instances of Mary's patience and modesty, her loyalty to her father and of the loving care and attention with which she had given him right up to the end. Tears filled the eyes of all who listened.

At this moment the Countess Amelia entered the drawing-room, holding Mary by one hand, and with the other carrying the basket of flowers. Everyone rushed to welcome Mary, who was overwhelmed with greetings and congratulations.

The Count took her kindly by the hand, and said "Poor child, how pale and thin you look! It was our inconsiderate conduct that deprived your cheeks of their fresh colour, and furrowed with wrinkles your brow which was formerly so smooth. We will spare no pains in order that the faded flowers may once more bloom on your cheeks. We banished you from your home; you shall have the house in future for your property. Your father enjoyed the pretty house and garden at Terborg as a tenant only, but now it shall be yours. My secretary will make out a deed of gift, and Amelia, who loves you so dearly, shall convey the gift to you with her own hands"

The Countess kissed Mary, pressed her to her heart, called her her daughter, and taking from her finger the ring which had caused so many misfortunes - "Here, my dear child," she said, "your truthfulness and love for God is a jewel more precious, it is true, than the large diamond which sparkles in this ring. Still, although you possess a richer treasure, accept this present - receive it as a feeble compensation for the wrong which you have suffered, and as a token of the love which I feel towards you. If the time should ever come when the price of the ring would be of more value to you than the jewel itself, come to me and I will redeem it from you at its full value."

With these words the Countess put the ring on Mary's finger.

Mary, who had shed so many bitter tears, now shed very sweet ones. She was quite overcome with the kindness shown to her, and was ready to sink under the weight of her sudden change of fortune, as though it was a heavy burden. She could scarcely speak for tears, but she implored the Countess not to ask her to take so rich a treasure.

"Poor child," said one of the two strangers, "take it. God has blessed the Count and his wife with the good things of this world, but he has given them something still more precious - hearts which know how to make the best use of their riches."

"Why do you flatter us?" said the Countess. "This is not a generous action - it is but an act of justice. We have done a great wrong to our poor friend, and it is only an act of Christian duty to undo that wrong and make compensation for it as far as we can."

Mary, always modest, held with a trembling hand the ring which she had taken, and turned her eyes, wet with tears, towards the pastor, as though to ask him what she should do.

"The Count and Countess wish you to accept this ring. Do not hesitate to accept it Mary," said the venerable minister. "Let this gift be an example of the way in which truly noble and upright minds endeavour to make amends for faults they have unknowingly committed. You see, my good child, God is blessing you. For whoever honours his parents shall be the better for it. God has promised it, and here God is using the Count and Countess to fulfil his word. Receive, then, their present with thanks."

Mary put the ring on her finger. She could hardly speak through her tears. Amelia, who stood beside her with the basket of flowers in her hand, was delighted with her parents generosity. Her eyes beamed with affection for Mary.

The minister, had only too often observed how envious children can be when their parents show kindness towards other people. However, he was touched by the love and care shown by Amelia. "May God," said he, "reward the generosity of the Count and Countess, and may all that they have done for a poor orphan be rendered to them a hundredfold, in the person of their own dear daughter. "And to be sure He will," he added after a pause; "for whatever of our worldly goods we devote to the good of our suffering fellow-creatures becomes pure gain to us. Not only are we rewarded in this world for our good deeds, but we are thereby, as we are told, laying up treasures in heaven which neither moth nor rust can corrupt, nor thieves take away."

Further Wonders of Providence

Supper was then served.And the Countess invited the pastor and Mary to eat with them. While grace was being said Mary breathed a prayer of thanks to God for his goodness. She could not help contrasting the position in which she now found herself, with a sumptuously-spread table before her, and what she had frequently of late experienced at Pine Farm, when she had often been obliged to go to bed hungry after a hard day's work. "How I thank you, Lord, for your loving care! Forgive my timidity, and give me thy grace, so that I will always be confident in you and trust in you in everything!"

Mary was shown to a seat between the Countess and her daughter; but she modestly held back and declined to take that place of honour. But the Countess said with a kindly smile: "Since you have been restored to us, it is fitting and proper that we should hold a feast, and at it you are entitled by right to the first place." Saying which she took Mary by the hand and led her to her seat.

During the meal little else was spoken of but Mary's story. The Count had brought with him the honest old huntsman Anthony. He assisted in waiting at his master's table and stood almost all the time behind Mary's chair, from time to time wiping a tear from his eye. By reason of his age and long service, he was often indulged to the extent of being allowed to mingle in the conversation.

He now said, respectfully addressing Mary, "Has it not proved true what I told you and your father in the forest, that honesty lasts the longest, and that he who trusts in God may be sure of divine protection? What joy it would have given your father to see you proved to all the world to be innocent. Why did he not live to see this day, and taste so great a pleasure?"

"Good old man," said the clergyman, "I admire your sentiments, for they do honour to your heart. But our view must not be limited by the short horizon of this life. The life we live upon earth is only a preparation for a better one, which is reserved for us in heaven. Now, if we consider the existence of man without regarding his future destination, we shall make a great mistake; but let us raise our eyes to heaven for consolation. That was the case with Mary and Jacob. The misfortunes that our young friend endured have already been recompensed in a most noble manner. As for her father, it was God's will that he should be plunged into the depths of misery, and die misjudged. But there is another and a better life. It is in heaven that the good man is rewarded for all his sufferings. There he tastes the joys of a glorious existence; and we who are seated at this banquet, in this brilliant room, have not a shadow of the pleasure he enjoys. But let me relate a fact which I had almost forgotten among so many other things.

"I went one morning to his bedside. He had been anxious about his dear daughter but that day I found him uncommonly cheerful. There was a smile on his lips. He held his hand out to me, and said, 'Now, sir,

I am at last freed from the burden that was on my heart - my anxiety concerning my daughter; I am now perfectly peaceful. Last night I prayed harder than I ever did in my life, and I felt my heart become calm. I felt utterly confident that my prayer had been heard. I shut my eyes and slept. I know that the innocence of my daughter will be discovered - the noble Count will take care of her as a father, and she will find a mother in the Countess.'

"That is what he said and this evening I have learned, to my great astonishment, it was that very night that the violence of the wind blew down the old tree which grew in the garden of the castle. It was then that the ring was discovered and the innocence of Mary shown to the whole world. Even at the very moment when Jacob prayed his prayer was answered. Even in heaven he now knows about the happiness of his daughter and is joyful.

Our meeting here is not an accident; or a result of blind chance. It is the goodness of God that has led us here. God overrules all things. We have a heavenly Father whose heart beats with love for us all. This belief is our only real comfort."

"That belief, my dear pastor," said the

Countess, rising, and giving him her hand, "I share with you."

Everyone now rose from the table.

"It is getting late," said the Countess, "and as we have to leave early tomorrow morning, we must rest a little. We could not have finished this day in a better manner."

All then bade each other good night, with hearts full of gratitude to God.

A Visit to Pine Farm

The next morning, as soon as the sun was up, everybody in the castle was busily occupied in making preparations for their departure; but busiest of all were the Countess Amelia and the young lady who was on a visit to the hunting lodge with her father, both of whom were doing their utmost to put Mary in a fit state to travel.

Mary had been used to dress as it was customary for those in the service of the gentry to do; but as during her residence at Pine Farm she had been obliged to buy her own clothes, she was able to get only those of the coarsest description, and she was therefore dressed almost exactly as the peasant girls of the neighbourhood.

But the young lady, who was of the same age and size as Mary, presented her, at the request of Amelia, with a complete dress, neat, handsome, new, and not too extravagant, which suited her new situation. "For," said Amelia, "henceforth you are my friend, my companion, and you will always live with me; therefore you must no longer dress like a country girl."

Mary gave her consent reluctantly at first. She would rather have retained her peasant dress. With the help of her kind young friends the transformation was soon made, and then the two young ladies descended with her to the breakfast room.

At first everyone was astonished to see three young ladies enter the room, but when they recognized Mary they hastened to congratulate her on the improved appearance she made in her new dress. After breakfast the carriage was ordered, and the whole party set out for a drive, Mary being seated beside Amelia, opposite to the Count and Countess. The Count ordered the coachman to take them at once to Pine Farm, as he wished to become acquainted with the people who had treated Mary and her father so kindly. On the way he inquired about their situation with great interest, and Mary did not hide from them that they were far from happy, and any prospect they had of enjoying comfort in their declining years was very remote.

The arrival of the carriage caused quite a stir at the cottage. Never since the existence of the farm, had a carriage - at least never so grand a one - appeared before its door.

No sooner had the young farmer's wife seen the carriage draw up, than she hastened out, saying that she must help the gentleman and lady and their two daughters to alight. Holding out her hand to one of the young ladies, she suddenly recognized Mary herself, and with an exclamation of surprise she let go her hand as if she had touched a serpent, drew back, and turned red and white by turns.

The old farmer was working in his garden. The Count, the Countess, and Amelia went to him, took him by the hand, and thanked him for his kindness to Mary and her father in the warmest terms.

"Ah!" said the honest peasant, "I owe that good old man more than he ever owed me. The blessing of heaven came with him into our house, and if I had followed his advice in everything, I should be much better for it at this moment. Since his death

I have no pleasure in anything but this garden. It is, besides, to his wise advice that I am indebted for reserving this little corner of ground, and from him I learned to cultivate it. Since I have not had strength to follow the plough, I have occupied myself here, and I seek among the herbs and flowers the peace that I no longer find in my house."

Meanwhile Mary had gone to look for the old farmer's wife in her little room, and she now came out into the garden, leading her by the hand, and desiring her not to be alarmed, for the good woman was quite overcome. She approached with a timid and embarrassed air, and was distressed to find herself overwhelmed with thanks.

The good old people were very much confused, and cried for joy. At last the farmer, addressing Mary, said, "My dear Mary, did I not tell you that your would receive your reward? Well, now is my prophecy fulfilled!"

Meanwhile the old woman, who had become a little encouraged by the kindness of the Count and Countess, said, as she ran her hand over Mary's dress, "Yes, yes! Your father was right- 'He who clothes the flowers knows how to take care of you'".

Their ill-natured daughter-in-law stood at some distance and said to herself, "Well, well! This miserable beggar - now look at her! - she is a young lady of high rank. Who would have thought of such a thing? There is not a woman in our town who can compare with her now. But everyone knows who she is - they know that yesterday she set out from here with her little package under her arm, to go and beg about the country."

The Count, of course, did not hear this abusive language, but he was disgusted with the mocking look and angry demeanour of the woman. "That is a wicked creature," he said; and he walked up and down the garden for some minutes in deep thought. At last, stopping before the farmer, he said, "Listen, I have a proposition. I have given Mary the little piece of ground which was cultivated by her father. But Mary is not yet ready to go into housekeeping. What is there to prevent you from going to live there? It will suit you, I am certain; and I know that the owner will not exact any rent from you. You can there cultivate as you choose herbs and flowers; and, above all, you will find in that pretty house both rest and peace in your old age."

The Count's wife, the Countess Amelia, and Mary, insisted that the old people should accept this offer. But there was no need of persuasion; for they were happy to be taken from their present uncomfortable situation. Just then the young farmer came home from the fields, and was anxious to know what had brought to his farm a carriage drawn by four white horses. The moment he knew what was proposed he consented to it, although it cost him a great deal to part with his parents. His greatest grief had been to see them so badly treated by his own wife, and it was a great consolation for him to think that they would be happier. The young wife was delighted at the prospect of getting rid of the old people. She said with an attempt at politeness, "It is most awfully kind of your excellence, and it would show great rudeness on our part if we did not accept your kindness. They are very difficult people to get on with, and they will, I am sure, be best by themselves. Indeed, it is a piece of great good luck for them to have such a chance!"

In his gratitude at seeing his parents so kindly provided for in their old age, the young farmer said, turning to his wife, "Did

I not always tell you that to show kindness to the poor brings blessings upon a house and happiness to its inmates? Perhaps you will confess that I was right."

The ill-natured wife flushed with anger. Suppressing her rage, however, in the presence of the Count and Countess, she cast a black look at her husband. He knew he would have to pay for his speech after they had gone.

The Count promised to send for the aged couple as soon as the necessary arrangements could be made to receive them in the cottage at Terborg, and after wishing them and their son and daughter-in-law good day, the party resumed their seats in the carriage and drove away.

A Contrast

The noble Count did not fail to keep his word.

In the autumn a carriage was sent from Terborg to Pine Farm to bring the two old people. The son wept bitterly when he saw that he was going to lose his father and mother. The daughter-in-law, however, who had counted the days and hours until the moment of their departure, felt the keenest joy at the prospect of being rid of them at last. However, before leaving, the coachman presented her with a legal document, ordering her husband, under penalty of a fine, to pay regularly every quarter a certain amount for the support and maintenance of his parents.

On reading this document, perceiving what it meant, the woman became violently angry. "If they had stayed here it would not have cost us half as much to keep them!" She stormed and threatened, and bade her husband not to let the old people go. But though he dared not say anything, the young farmer was secretly glad at the turn things had taken. He took great care, however, not to show his joy. The good people set off in the carriage the next morning, with the blessings of their son, and the secret ill wishes of their daughter-in-law.

This wicked woman had the fate she deserved. It is always the lot of greed and inhumanity. She had placed her money in the hands of a merchant who had just set up a manufactory, and who had promised to pay her ten per cent interest. The annual interest was added to the capital, which produced a new interest, and so on each year. The farmer's wife thought herself the happiest of women, and had no greater pleasure in the world than to make calculations of the sum to which all this money would amount in ten and in twenty years. But all this suddenly changed for the worse.

The enterprise of the merchant did not succeed, and his goods were sold by order of the sheriff. This was a thunder-stroke for the farmer's wife. From the moment she heard of this catastrophe she no longer enjoyed any rest. She was seen almost all day either on the road running to see her lawyer or else at one or other of her neighbours' complaining of her hardships. Generally she spent the night in weeping and scolding. Instead of her ten thousand dollars, she received some hundreds. The blow was so severe to the greedy woman that she gave in to despair; life became a torture to her, and she wished for death. Weakened and worn out with her worries, she was at length attacked with a fever which never left her. Her husband wished to go for the physician of the village, but she would not consent to it. For once the young farmer resisted, and sent for the doctor; but his wife in a passion, threw the medicine out of the window, without even uncorking the bottle.

At last she became so seriously ill that her husband requested the pastor of Erlenbrunn to come and see her. He did so frequently during her sickness, and talked to her in the most persuasive tones in the hope that she might be persuaded to repent and amend her ways - to detach her heart from the things of this earth, and to turn to God. But this advice made her very angry; she looked at the good minister with utter astonishment.

"I do not know," said she, "for what purpose the clergyman comes to preach repentance to me. He ought to have delivered his sermon to the merchant who defrauded us of our money. As for me, I do not see that I have any great need of repentance. So long as I was able to go out I went regularly to church on Sunday, and at home I never failed to say my prayers every day. I have not ceased to work hard all my life. I defy anyone to slander me. Among all the poor people who came to my door, not one of them can complain that I sent him away without giving him something. Now I should like to know how any one can behave better? I should have thought that the pastor would have considered me one of the most pious and virtuous people of all his parish."

The pastor was obliged to take a more urgent tone with the farmer's wife. He showed her in the most unmistakable manner, that she loved money more than anything in the world, and that greed is in fact nothing but idolaltry. He pointed out how she was prone to fits of anger and bad temper. These were also sins. She hadn't even shown love to her own family members and with her greed and selfishness she had poisoned the days of her husband, cruelly driven away the poor orphan Mary, and even turned out of her house her husband's aged parents, whom she ought to have cherished and honoured as if they were her own.

He convinced her too that she had failed in her duty of charitable giving. With her sizable fortune she could easily have given more than she did. She knew nothing of true love to man, founded on a sincere love of God. Despite all her boasting of going to church, public worship could not save her soul. Prayers coming from a heart unwarmed by love, were far from being true prayers.

However when the pastor had gone on for some time she stopped him and refused to listen any more. Then she began to sob and cry through passion.

The good pastor, quite troubled, took his hat and cane and went away. "Alas!" said he, "how difficult it is for a heart set upon things of this world to look forward to those of heaven! How far is such a heart from the kingdom of God! It considers itself excused before God by repetition of a few vain words and prayers. They think that their duty towards their neighbour means throwing them a few crumbs. These people in their blindness mistake greed for virtue." As the pastor passed by the garden he remembered Mary and her flowers. 'How wrong some people are in supposing that to be rich is to be happy! This farmer's rich wife, with all her money and all her goods, was never as happy as poor Mary was amidst the flowers of this garden."

However, the farmer's wife had yet much to suffer. She spent whole nights coughing. She was utterly unwilling to submit to God and his will. The good pastor tried in every imaginable way to bring her to a better frame of mind. Occasionally she appeared a little softened during the last days of her life, but she never showed true repentance. At last she died, still a young woman. An awful picture of the effects of greed, selfishness, and love of the things of this world.

A Late Repentance

After a while Mary went with the Count's family to the city in which he resided part of the year. While there, an old clergyman came one morning to the Count's residence and asked to see Mary. He told her he came from a person who was very ill, and near death's door, and who desired to speak with Mary before she died. He added that the person could not die in peace, unless this favour was granted, and that she was not willing to speak to anyone except Mary.

This strange request astonished Mary very much; she consulted the Countess as to what she ought to do. The Countess, who knew the clergyman to be a pious and prudent man, advised her to go with him. At the request of the clergyman, old Anthony accompanied them.

They had a long way to go, the area to which the clergyman led them being in a remote district of one of the suburbs. At last they arrived in front of a house situated in a gloomy side street. There were five flights of stairs to climb, the last two of which were so dark, so narrow, and so broken that Mary was almost overcome with fear.

The clergyman stopped before a roughly hewn door. "This is the place," said he; "but wait a little."

He went in for a moment, and then returned for Mary, who was shown into a most miserable little attic. The window was narrow and dark, and the panes were filled with paper. A broken truckle bed covered with a straw mattress, a broken chair, and a stone pitcher with neither handle nor cover, composed the furniture. The patient stretched on the bed was truly a frightful object. Mary thought she saw a skeleton move and begin to speak with a frightful voice, which resembled the death-rattle more than anything else. The skeleton extended to her a hand which seemed nothing but skin and bone.

Mary trembled in every limb, and it was with great difficulty that at last she learned, by the indistinct words pronounced with difficulty, that this sad spectacle was - Juliette! - Juliette, who, at the castle, had been the cause of all her distress. This wretched woman had learned from the minister that Mary was in the city with the family of the Count; and she wished to see her to ask her pardon for the wrong she had done her. She had begged the clergyman not to mention her name, being afraid that Mary, justly irritated, might refuse to come.

Mary felt near to tears. She assured Juliette that all, absolutely all, was forgiven a long time ago, and that the only feeling she experienced was pity.

"Alas!" said Juliette, "I am a great sinner; I have deserved my fate. Forgetfulness of God - contempt of good advice. Instead I loved nothing but clothes and flattery and pleasure. But these have only brought me misery, and this it is which has brought me so low. Oh!" she cried, raising her voice and weeping bitterly, "I fear a still worse fate awaits me in the world to come! You have forgiven me - you whom I so cruelly injured; but I feel the weight of God's displeasure."

Mary had a long conversation with Juliette, and tried to turn her to the precious Saviour, who would receive her if she would repent; but she was obliged to leave her without knowing what Juliette felt. The idea of the sinful Juliette perishing without hope continually weighed on her mind, and affected her spirits. The sad appearance of the once beautiful girl was ever present in her thoughts. Then she remembered her little apple-tree in blossom withered by the frost, and what her father had said to her on that occasion. She also remembered the consoling words he had said on his deathbed and she renewed the promise she had made to God, to live entirely to his glory. She remembered the words of Jesus Christ, "Do good to them that hate you, and pray for them who despitefully use you and persecute you."

Under these feelings she begged the Countess to relieve Juliette's distress. The generous lady sent her medicine, food, linen, everything she needed. But it was all too late. At the age of twenty-three she died. She gave no evidence of repentance, but died as she had lived - without God and without hope.

Mary's Return to Terborg

The next spring, when the country was covered with greenery and flowers, the Count, accompanied by his wife and daughter, returned to the castle. Mary accompanied them, and took her accustomed place in the carriage by the side of Amelia. Towards the evening, as they approached Terborg, Mary caught sight of the tower of the church all aglow in the light of the setting sun, the gleaming windows of the castle, and her father's house, and was deeply moved. "When I left here how little I expected ever to return, and least of all in such joy and honour! How mysterious are the ways of God, and how good he is!"

When the carriage drew up at the door of the castle, all those in service of the

Count, not only the servants, but the higher officials connected with the estate, stood in readiness to receive the family with all due ceremony and respect.

Mary had a most flattering reception. Everyone showed great joy at seeing her again. The old judge who had condemned her took her hand with great tenderness, and asked for forgiveness in front of everyone for the part he had taken in her condemnation and punishment. He at the same time expressed his gratitude to the Count and Countess for trying to make amends for the injustice committed. He said that he also was only too anxious to do all in his power to pay the debt he had unwittingly incurred.

The following morning Mary rose very early. She hurriedly got dressed and hastened out into the morning to visit the beloved house in which she had been born. She longed to look once again at the garden in which she had spent so many happy hours. On her way she met none but friendly faces; many of them belonged to young people to whom in their infancy she had been in the habit of giving flowers, but who had grown so much that she hardly knew them.

The old farmer and his wife, who had now been livng in the house for some time, came out to meet her, kissed her affectionately, and told her how happily and contentedly they lived. Tears of joy were in the farmer's eyes. "When you were without a home," he said, "we received you under our roof; and now that we are turned out of our own house, you give us this beautiful cottage to live in."

"Yes," said his wife, "it is always best to be hospitable and kind to others; we know not how soon they may be in a position to help us in return."

"That is true," answered the old man, "but we did not think of that then, and were not influenced by such a thought. However, it is true that if we do good to others, we shall always find some to do good to us."

Mary entered the house. The sight of the room - the place where her father used to sit - awoke sad memories. She walked round the garden greeting every tree planted by her father, as though in each one she saw again an old acquaintance; but she stopped particularly before the little apple-tree, then all covered with beautiful blossoms. Sighing she said "Life is so short! Even the trees and shrubs survive us."

Finally she made her way to the arbour where she had passed so many happy days with her father. As she sat there and looked round the garden which he had cultivated, it was almost as though she could see him going to and fro as he used to. But one thought soothed her heart. Her father was now in a far better place.

Mary remained as companion to Countess Amelia, and each spring returned with the Count's family to spend a few weeks at Terborg, where she was honoured and beloved by everyone. One morning she and Amelia were busily engaged in their little work-room finishing a dress they were making. While thus employed they were surprised to receive a visit from the old judge. It was evident from the fact that he was dressed in official garb that his business was of great importance. Amelia and Mary looked at each other, and wondered what could be the meaning of this ceremonious visit. The worthy gentleman did not leave them long in doubt. After showing his respect to the young Countess, he said that he had a proposal of great importance to make to

Mary. Amelia at once rose and left the room, so that the judge might speak to Mary alone.

He at once turned to Mary and told her that he came on behalf of his son Frederick, who had long admired her for her goodness of heart and her many other noble qualities, and who the previous day had informed him of his inclination, and his desire, if possible, to make her his wife. The worthy judge added that, like a good and obedient son, Frederick had been unwilling to make known his affection to her and his wish without first obtaining the consent of his father to do so. This consent he not only gave at once, but gladly undertook to speak to Mary on his son's behalf. With her permission he would lay the matter before the Count and Countess. He went on to say that the union, if it could be brought about, would be doubly pleasing to him because of the wrong he had unwittingly done her. It had been committed, he said, in the discharge of his duty, but that fact had not eased his troubled conscience. If Mary could see her way to accept the offer he made in his son's name, he should look upon their marriage as in some measure making amends for the pain he had caused her.

Mary's confusion and blushes became deeper and deeper as the judge spoke, and she could not at first command herself sufficiently to answer him. The fact is, that she had long had a secret liking for the young man, who was not only of an excellent disposition, but had great natural ability. He was also very good-looking. Since Mary's return they had often met, and from time to time had talked together in the garden of the castle. From the first she had noticed his liking for her. But as soon as she perceived that her thoughts were inclining towards him she checked herself, and avoided coming in contact with him as much as possible. She considered herself unworthy of the young man and desired to spare herself the pain of allowing a feeling to grow in her heart which would only torment her. She tried, therefore, to think as little of him as possible.

But now Mary blushed while replying to the judge. Stammering she said how she felt herself greatly honoured by the judge's proposal, but that it had taken her so much by surprise that she must have time to consider the matter. She must also consult the Count and Countess, who had been like father and mother to her.

This was quite enough for the wise judge, who at once took his leave. He was very happy. He had seen that Mary's affection was with his son, and he had no doubt that the marriage would be agreeable to the Count and Countess. Going to them immediately he asked their approval.

They were both highly pleased. The Count, who was the first to speak, said, "You bring us a great news. The Countess and I have often noticed the attraction that exists between your son and our beloved Mary, and have remarked how well adapted they are to each other. We were careful, however, not to show that we noticed anything. We feared that our wishes might be mistaken for a command, which would have been very disagreeable. It is, therefore, all the more pleasing to us that our wishes have been fulfilled without any interference on our part."

"I do congratulate you," said the Countess. "A better daughter-in-law than Mary you could not have, nor your son a better wife. Mary has been taught in the school of adversity, which is the best of all schools and has a meek and humble heart.

She has never been spoiled by flattery. She is the most modest and the most unassuming little body I know; and, what is best of all, she is truly and sincerely pious. She has been trained to work hard and no one could know better how to manage a household than she does. During her stay with us in the capital she has acquired a real grace and polish necessary in good society. Indeed, you will find her in every respect a perfect lady, and your son will be a fortunate man if he marries her."

As soon as the Countess had learned from Mary that she was ready to fall in with the judge's proposal, she began to make the arrangements for the wedding. She took everything upon herself, including the purchase and preparation of the trousseau. It was decided that Mary should be married from the castle, and that the wedding breakfast should be given there. The Countess could not have thrown herself into the affair with more heart if it had been her own daughter who was to be married.

"How nice it would be," she exclaimed, with a smile, "for Mary to wear the ring - the very ring which caused her so much sorrow - as her wedding ring! What could be more appropriate?"

It was also decided that the pastor of Erlenbrunn should be invited to perform the marriage ceremony.

The wedding-day was the most festive that had ever been known in the countryside. The whole of the Count's family arrived at the church, which was crowded to the very door by the people of the village and neighbourhood. Everyone was eager to do honour to a bride who, though she had suffered imprisonment and chains, had risen to such distinction.

The bride looked the picture of beauty and modesty in her white wreath and veil, whilst the young Countess Amelia was the loveliest of bridesmaids. The old huntsman, Anthony, was present with the rest, and he could not help contrasting the position of the bride, the dutiful daughter of his old friend, with that of Juliette, to whose lodgings he had accompanied Mary.

The good pastor referred to Mary's father. Holding up his method of educating his daughter as a model to parents of the way in which children should be trained to piety and right living. He also pointed to Mary as an example to the young, showing how love and obedience are the beginning of all virtue.

The wedding breakfast, which was held in the great hall of the castle, was a magnificent affair, and filled everyone with delight. Next to the bride, who sat so modestly, and looked so beautiful, by the side of the handsome bride-groom, the object that attracted most attention was the basket of flowers, which Amelia had secretly filled with the most beautiful flowers. This was placed in the centre of the table. The pastor was especially struck by it, and by the happy forethought of the young Countess in placing it there. In the little speech which he was called upon to make after the breakfast, he suggested that Mary should preserve it as a precious heirloom, to remind her at all times of the increasing goodness and watchfulness of God.

The Monument

Meanwhile the monument which Amelia had promised Mary would be raised to the memory of her father had been finished. It was a very simple and beautiful construction of white marble, with an epitaph in gilt letters. To the name of the deceased, his age, and his double profession of gardener and basket-maker, nothing had been added but these words of Jesus, which certainly deserved to be engraven in letters of gold - "I am the resurrection and the life; he that believeth in me, though he were dead, yet shall he live."

Underneath a skilful workman had cut the figure of the basket, which the Lord had made use of in delivering Mary from her trouble. Amelia had drawn the basket, after it had been filled by Mary's hand with the most beautiful flowers, and the drawing, which was a striking resemblance, was copied by the craftsman. Beneath the basket was written this text from the holy scripture, "All flesh is grass, and all the goodliness thereof as the flower of the field. The grass withereth, the flower fadeth, but the word of the Lord endureth for ever."

It was with great pleasure that the good pastor of Erlenbrunn, Mary's early friend, had the monument erected on Jacob's grave. It had an imposing effect amid the dark foliage of the pines. When the rose-tree, growing on the grave, was in bloom, and the green branches covered with roses, bent over the dazzling white marble, nothing could be more beautiful. The monument was the most striking ornament of the churchyard, and the chief attraction of the village.

The pastor never failed to point it out to strangers who came to the village. Many observed that it was a good idea to put a basket of flowers on the tomb of a man who was once a gardener and a basket-maker.

"Ah!" the pastor would reply, "it is